JOSEPH

The Carpenter from Nazareth

Carol
God Bless!
Frank Durham

FRANK DURHAM

WestBow Press
A DIVISION OF THOMAS NELSON
& ZONDERVAN

Copyright © 2015 Frank Durham.

All rights reserved. No part of this book may be used or reproduced by any means, graphic, electronic, or mechanical, including photocopying, recording, taping or by any information storage retrieval system without the written permission of the publisher except in the case of brief quotations embodied in critical articles and reviews.

Cover Design by Gregory A Durham

Scripture taken from the Holy Bible, NEW INTERNATIONAL VERSION®. Copyright © 1973, 1978, 1984 by Biblica, Inc. All rights reserved worldwide. Used by permission. NEW INTERNATIONAL VERSION® and NIV® are registered trademarks of Biblica, Inc. Use of either trademark for the offering of goods or services requires the prior written consent of Biblica US, Inc.

This is a work of fiction. All of the characters, names, incidents, organizations, and dialogue in this novel are either the products of the author's imagination or are used fictitiously.

WestBow Press books may be ordered through booksellers or by contacting:

WestBow Press
A Division of Thomas Nelson & Zondervan
1663 Liberty Drive
Bloomington, IN 47403
www.westbowpress.com
1 (866) 928-1240

Because of the dynamic nature of the Internet, any web addresses or links contained in this book may have changed since publication and may no longer be valid. The views expressed in this work are solely those of the author and do not necessarily reflect the views of the publisher, and the publisher hereby disclaims any responsibility for them.

Any people depicted in stock imagery provided by Thinkstock are models, and such images are being used for illustrative purposes only.
Certain stock imagery © Thinkstock.

ISBN: 978-1-4908-7985-7 (sc)
ISBN: 978-1-4908-7986-4 (hc)
ISBN: 978-1-4908-7984-0 (e)

Library of Congress Control Number: 2015907291

Print information available on the last page.

WestBow Press rev. date: 6/22/2015

I dedicate this book to my wife,
Shirley.
Who, after sixty-two years of marriage, still blesses me with her love.

Contents

Acknowledgments ix
Introduction xi

1. Joseph and Mary 1
2. Gabriel Visits Mary 9
3. Mary Explains 15
4. Joseph's Prayer 30
5. Days Pass Slowly 34
6. New Neighbors 36
7. News about Mary 43
8. Mary's Return 46
9. Their New Home 51
10. They Go Exploring 55
11. Meeting Neighbors 59
12. Trip to Bethlehem 62
13. Joseph Delivers the Messiah 69

14. Fulfilling Jewish Laws............................ 76
15. Three Magi Visit 82
16. They Flee to Egypt 85
17. Life in Goshen, Egypt........................... 94
18. Jesus' First Birthday............................100
19. Return to Israel 103
20. Home Again.....................................111
21. They Are Inseparable 118
22. Mary's Announcement........................121
23. A Son for Joseph 124
24. Jesus Explores the Hills 127
25. As The Family Grows, Jesus Matures.............129
26. Jesus' World Expands 134
27. Passover in Jerusalem 137
28. The Family Increases 142
29. Anna, Judas, and Sarah, Complete the Family 147
30. Jesus Grows Spiritually.......................149
31. Joseph Was Obedient 153
32. Jesus Guides the Family 158
33. Jesus Leaves.....................................161

Closing Comments...................................165

Acknowledgments

A special thank you to my wife, Shirley, for being so patient with me during the many months of writing and publishing this book … I love you.

To my talented son, Dr. Gregg Durham, who created the cover. It is beautiful! I'm proud of you.

I am so grateful for the encouragement and suggestions I received from my friends Shirley Brown and Charlie and Mary Jane Miller. You spent a lot of time proofreading this book.

Pastor Scott Jones, thank you for suggesting that we, as Ironmen, should write our Jesus stories.

To the people at West Bow Press, especially Jenn Seiler, you helped this old man publish a book. Wow!

Finally, thank you to my niece, Debra Durham, who insisted that it be published. I am in your debt.

Introduction

The story I have written is about Joseph, Jesus' earthly father. If you were to search the Scriptures, you would find very little written about him. He is mentioned in only five verses of Scripture as being engaged to Mary, being the husband of Mary, and being a carpenter. In three other verses of Scripture, an angel speaks to him in a dream, but at no time does he speak.

However, the time span covered in Scripture where Joseph is involved is from Jesus' birth until he is twelve years old. After that, there is no mention of Joseph. But Scripture does record that he and Mary had four sons and at least two daughters. If that is the case, then Jesus must have been about twenty-four years old when Joseph died.

Also, when we read Scripture, the gospel writers are reporting the facts with little or no personal detail. Therefore I enjoy taking these verses of Scripture and building a personal account of what I think may have happened.

I also feel that Joseph was much younger than depicted by artists. I believe that he and Mary's marriage was predestined by God and they fell in love at first sight and their lives were a love story where they were always obedient to God.

However, it is not my intention to change the gospel story. What I have written is purely my own ideas and thoughts on how such a love story might have happened.

CHAPTER 1

Joseph and Mary

Nestled on top of a hill, with a commanding view of the Jezreel Valley to the southeast and Mount Hermon to the north, sits the village of Nazareth, a community of about five hundred people. Because of its strategic view of the area, it was considered an important military outpost several centuries ago, but now it is a Roman garrison for the area of Galilee.

It is a peaceful village except when a few Jewish zealots become upset with the Roman soldiers and challenge them. This generally happens when a legion of soldiers passes by on its way to Jerusalem. Because it is located at the crossroads of major caravan trade routes, the local residents receive up-to-date world news as well as economic benefits from the caravan traders who visit the local vendors to replenish their food and supplies.

The local citizens are hardworking and loyal to their faith. They rarely venture far from their homes except to visit family and friends in nearby villages or when they make their required pilgrimage to the temple in Jerusalem to celebrate the Passover and other religious festivals.

It is also the home of Joseph, a young carpenter who was born in Bethlehem but has spent most of his life here. He is betrothed to Mary, who also lives in Nazareth.

In his youth, Joseph and his friends would explore the nearby hills dotted with olive and date groves. Nearby, to the northwest, is the town of Sepphoris. Just a very short distance east of it is Cana, and to the south of Nazareth is a larger town called Japha. These communities, along with his hometown, provide a market for Joseph's farm tools and furniture he builds in his carpentry workshop.

Now that the late spring rains are over, the hills and countryside outside of Nazareth are alive with color. Poppies, phlox, and lupine reach for the warm sunshine. They blanket the slopes of the hills, adding a beauty the townspeople look forward to every year.

It is early morning in the village, and the merchants are busy waiting on the women who have come to purchase their wares. The food vendors are also anticipating a good day of sales, and most of the women have already been to the village well for their daily water supply. Those who linger enjoy visiting with friends and catching up on the latest news while their children play nearby. In the meantime, the men are busy tending their crops in the fields or are grooming the olive and date groves.

Inside the synagogue, small boys sit cross-legged on the floor at the feet of Rabbi Levi, learning the law of Moses. Over and over they recite them. If they learn them well, they can read them in the synagogue services when they grow up. But outside, the sunshine and warm air on the hills call them to play. For now though, they must remain attentive to the rabbi's droning voice.

Meanwhile, across town, a young girl named Mary, the daughter of Joachim and Anna, has just returned home from the village well with a jar of water. After placing the jar on the table, she sits down to cool off from her long walk home through the warm, narrow streets. Just then her mother, Anna, enters the room.

Anna finds a chair near Mary, and they both pick up their sewing and start mending clothes. Shortly into their project, Anna notices that Mary seems to be preoccupied with her private thoughts, so she asks, "Mary, aren't you feeling well?"

"I'm fine, Mother," Mary answers. "I just feel the need for some quiet time."

"I too have those moments and have found that I'm better able to resolve my problems when I'm alone up on the roof. Why don't you take your sewing up there? The privacy and warm sun will help you feel better."

"I believe I will, and thank you for suggesting it, Mother." Mary picks up her sewing and heads for the outside stairway.

When she arrives on the roof, she sits down on a soft rug and starts to sew. In a little while, she is feeling better. The warm spring sun and a gentle breeze calm her.

As she sits quietly sewing, her thoughts shift back and forth between her upcoming marriage to Joseph and an indescribable feeling of euphoria. Never before has she felt this contented—this spiritually satisfied. She can only compare it to the love she receives from her mother and father.

Mary truly is enjoying her quiet time alone on the roof.

Meanwhile, on the opposite side of town, it is still early morning, and Joseph is in his workshop. Because it is a warm day, he has the window and door open.

He is busy building a cabinet for his friends Amos and Rachel, who were recently married and are furnishing their new home. He has just fitted the final piece in place and does not hear his mother, Miriam, enter.

"Joseph," she calls to him, "dinner is ready. Come, wash up, eat, and then rest for a while. You have been working on that cabinet since early dawn."

"I'll be in shortly, Mother," he says. "It will only take me a moment to secure this last piece, and then it will be ready to be oiled and rubbed down."

As Miriam turns to leave, she pauses for a moment to take in the pleasant smell of sawdust and wood shavings that permeates the shop. Then she admires the cabinet Joseph is finishing. It reminds her of the many beautiful pieces he has made for her.

A few minutes later she hears him washing at the bench just outside of his shop. She and Jacob sit down at the table as Joseph enters the house. After greeting his father, he hugs his mother and quietly sits down as Jacob offers the blessing.

As they are eating, Joseph turns to his father and asks, " This afternoon would you help me load the cabinet on the cart? I need to deliver it to Amos and Rachel this afternoon."

"Yes, I can help," Jacob replies. "I'm anxious to see it. Your mother says it's beautiful. Will you need help delivering it?"

"No, I can handle it, but thank you. I'm happy with the way it turned out. Also, I plan to stop by and see Mary. We have some final wedding plans to make, so I may be late getting back."

With that, Jacob asks, "Have you decided to rent the house you looked at last week?"

"That is one of the things that Mary and I will be discussing, along with setting the date."

It is midafternoon before Joseph and his father get the cabinet loaded and secured on the cart. Then Joseph and the donkey, which he calls Abner, head for Amos's house.

As Joseph travels through the village square, a number of people greet him, stopping him to admire the cabinet. Before he can continue on, he is asked to build one for Nathan and his wife, Ruth.

"I will stop by your home soon, and you can tell me what type of wood and finish you want on it," he tells them.

"That will be fine," Ruth says. "I can hardly wait to have one of my own."

"I'll see you in a few days," Joseph responds as he resumes his journey through the narrow streets.

But as he turns the corner, only a short distance from Amos's house, he pauses to look at the neighborhood and admires the small, comfortable homes. They remind him of the house that he and Mary looked at and are considering to rent. He can almost see in his mind what it will be like inside their home with Mary and several children.

However, he will need to build a small stable and a workshop, which he is looking forward to, and of course the roof will be a perfect place where they can all rest in the evening and enjoy the cool night air and also the view overlooking the village.

After collecting his thoughts, he continues down the street and knocks on his friend's door. While Joseph is securing Abner, Amos rushes out, and together they carry the new cabinet inside.

Rachel is so pleased with it that she hurries to gather all the items she planned to store in it. After arranging the items, she steps back and admires the cabinet.

She returns to Joseph and asks, "How is Mary? I miss her since we moved to our new home. We must get together soon."

"She is fine, and I'm on my way to see her now. I will tell her you asked of her."

They then say their good-byes and promise to get together soon.

CHAPTER 2

Gabriel Visits Mary

It is now very late afternoon as Joseph guides Abner through the winding, narrow streets. The shadows are growing longer, and the sky begins to show God's glory by sending out orange and yellow hues reflecting off the clouds overhead as the sun begins to set.

The shops are closing, and families are gathering in their homes when Joseph arrives at Mary's house. After he ties Abner up to a post, he knocks on Mary's door. For some reason there is no noise coming from inside the house, and Mary doesn't answer the door. After waiting a moment, he goes around the house to the back and she is not there either, so this leaves the roof.

He climbs the outside stairway, and there he finds her, sitting on a soft rug looking out over the village as if she too were enjoying the sunset. Softly he calls her name, "*Mary,*" but there is no reply as he moves around in front of her.

Still there is no response, but it is then that Joseph notices a beautiful radiance about her that he had never seen before. She has a look of angelic brilliance that is beyond description. He quietly sits down beside her, and as he takes her hand in his, a soft breeze gently brushes across her face, ruffling her hair. Joseph still cannot believe her beauty, and he silently thanks God for giving her to be his wife.

Finally, Mary is aware of Joseph's presence as she smiles and leans her head against his chest, but she is lost for words to describe what has happened to her and how she feels. However, Joseph is content to hold her close as she assures him that she is fine.

As the silence continues, they watch the day turn to night, and the sky comes alive, with gem-like stars shining bright while the crescent moon slips behind a small cloud.

When the night air becomes chilly, Joseph turns to her and says, "It's time for me to go. Let me help you down the stairs. I will come by tomorrow, and maybe then you'll be able to tell me what happened today that makes you so angelic looking."

He gently takes her by the hand, and they descend the stairway, where they pause for a moment at her door. They embrace, and he says, "Good night. I will return tomorrow."

Mary responds with a tender kiss on Joseph's cheek and a smile before she turns and enters the house.

Joseph unhitches Abner from the post and starts for home, but he remembers little of the journey. His thoughts are still with Mary, and he wonders what happened to her that suddenly made her so radiant looking.

When he arrives home, he unhitches Abner and rolls the cart into the corner of the stable. Then he gently guides the animal into his stall. After filling Abner's feed bag with oats, he fills the small trough with water. But before leaving the stable, he stops and rubs Abner down with a brush as he gently talks to him. Joseph is very fond of this animal. Although he is young, he is strong, he learns fast, and he is very loyal. With a pat on Abner's rump, Joseph heads into the house.

After telling his parents that he is home, Joseph has too much on his mind to go directly to bed, so he goes outside and climbs the stairs to the roof. It is here, away from the distractions of everyday life that he feels close to God. It is here, with God's help, that he is able to work through his problems.

However, tonight his thoughts are on Mary and how indescribably beautiful she looked. Joseph cannot for the life of him understand what might have happened that caused her to be so unresponsive yet so contented with her surroundings. It seemed like she was in a supernatural trance.

As he reflects on and prays about Mary's actions and appearance, he cannot help but recall how he and Mary first discovered each other. Even though Joseph knows that all marriages are arranged by parents, he can't help but feel that God played a big part in theirs.

He recalls that it was a warm summer day when he was passing by the village square that he first saw her. She had just filled her jar with water at the well and was turning to leave when they nearly bumped into one another. Immediately, their eyes locked on each other, and they could only smile and step aside. But in that moment something registered in their emotions that neither one could comprehend. As awkward as it seemed at the time, they both felt that it was predestined that they would meet.

Joseph realized that Mary was still a young girl of about twelve years old and he was sixteen, but there was something that spoke to their souls that they could not explain. As time passed, neither one spoke to the other unless they were with their parents. However, they both knew they were very fond of each other.

In the following years, Joseph enjoyed watching Mary grow and mature into a young woman. While they both treasured any opportunity that presented itself for them to be together, at all times they were chaperoned. However, they would often see each other on the Sabbath at the synagogue or at religious festivals, when they were with family, and then they would talk briefly.

Only on rare occasions did they happen to meet privately and share their real feelings toward each other. As a result of this, they hoped their parents would understand their desire to wed. This became their prayer, and to their joy it happened. Now they are planning their wedding.

But what happened today? Joseph ponders as he closes his prayer by praising God and promising to continue to be obedient.

After a few minutes of enjoying the beauty of the night sky and the view of the village from the rooftop, Joseph realizes he is tired and heads down to his bed.

CHAPTER 3

Mary Explains

The next morning as Joseph slowly wakes up, the sun is shining through his open window, and he can see the dust particles sparkling in the rays.

Quietly, he dresses and goes out to the stable, and after he cleans it, he refills Abner's feed bag with more oats and fills the water trough. Joseph leads Abner out to the pen, saying, "You can just rest and graze and enjoy the shade because I have no work for you today."

When Joseph returns to the house, his mother and father are both up, so he sits down and eats with them and tells them that he plans to return to Mary's house after he cleans and reorganizes his shop. He says nothing about last night and how Mary looked because even he is not sure how to explain it.

It is midmorning when he finishes his work in the shop and heads for the house to clean up before he leaves to see Mary. He's soon on his way, and when he arrives, he inquires of Joachim and Anna as to Mary's whereabouts. They tell him she is up on the roof.

But before he can leave, they ask him, "Do you know what happened yesterday to Mary that has changed her so?"

"No, I don't, but I hope she's able to explain it to me today," he responds as he turns to head for the roof.

Joseph finds her there quietly sitting on a rug, and he notices that her countenance has returned to near normal as they sit facing one another.

As Mary reaches out and takes his hands in hers, she says, "Joseph, I prayed most of last night, asking God to give me the words to tell you what I experienced yesterday afternoon, and in my prayer I recalled how we met and how we have always felt that God arranged our meeting. So please be patient with me as I recall everything that happened, and I think then you'll see His plan for us."

Joseph nods in agreement as she starts to tell about what happened.

She briefly closes her eyes to recall what the setting was like and then opens them and smiles at Joseph. "The most amazing thing happened as I was quietly sitting alone in the house sewing yesterday. All of a sudden a beautiful bright light, like I have never seen before, filled the room. At first I thought that I might be dreaming so I looked around the room and saw where I had just laid my sewing, and my shawl was hung on the peg, so I knew I was not dreaming.

"The angel Gabriel appeared and started to speak, saying, 'Greetings, you who are highly favored! The Lord is with you.'

"Oh, Joseph, I was just as confused and was trying very hard to understand the meaning of this, just as you are right now."

After another brief pause, she continues. "Then the angel said to me, 'Do not be afraid, Mary. You have found favor with God. You will be with child and give birth to a son, and you are to give him the name Jesus. He will be great and will be called the Son of the Most High. The Lord God will give him the throne of his father David, and he will reign over the house of Jacob forever; his kingdom will never end.'

"Joseph, I was confused so I asked the angel, 'How will this be, since I am a virgin?'

"Then the angel told me, 'The Holy Spirit will come upon you, and the power of the Most High will overshadow you. So the holy one to be born will be called the Son of God.'"

There is a long pause as Mary looks at him with concern, for she knows Joseph is still confused. Mary then takes Joseph's hand and says, "My response to the angel was, 'I am the Lord's servant. May it be to me as you have said.'"

Then the questions just erupt from Joseph's mouth. "You saw an angel? And he said you would be with child? What does this Son of the Mo-Mo-Most High mean?" He stammers as his mind spins faster than he can speak.

For a short time, he looks away from her, still struggling with his thoughts. *An angel talked to you? You're with child? Son of whom?* He keeps saying these things over and over to himself. Then he turns and looks at Mary again.

"Yes, Joseph, I'm with child," she says, "I've been blessed by God," she whispers, hoping it will ease his mind.

"Mary, Mary," he whispers back to her. "I have so many feelings and thoughts going through my mind now that I don't know where to start."

There is another long silence between them as they sit quietly. "I think I need some time to think about what this means to our plans and what this means to our relationship from now on," he says.

Quietly, Mary bows her head and knows that Joseph is experiencing the same confusion that gripped her at first yesterday. But today she feels a wholeness and peace like she has never had before.

She is also aware that Joseph needs some time to think this through, so very tenderly she reaches out with her hand and lifts his chin so she can look into his eyes and says with all her heart, "Joseph, always remember that I love you very much, and this is God's plan, and I am his servant."

For a few minutes they sit quietly until Mary once again says to him, "There was one more thing that the angel told me, and that is that my cousin, Elizabeth, who is in her old age, and said to be barren, is six months pregnant, and I need to go to her and help her in her final months."

Once again, this causes Joseph to try to work his mind through the ramification of Mary's comments. Then he asks her, "Doesn't she live in Hebron, which is a five-day journey from here?"

"Yes, but it is very important that I go," she says, knowing Joseph is concerned about her safety. "And I must leave day after tomorrow."

By now, Joseph doesn't know how to respond to anything Mary has said to him, so the silence continues.

Finally Joseph says, "It's beginning to get warm here on the roof. We should go back down to the ground and seek some shade."

In the shade of a fig tree, Joseph says softly to Mary, "I must return home now, but I will call on you again tomorrow." With that, they embrace, and Joseph turns and slowly walks away with a heavy, aching feeling in his heart.

As Mary watches him go, she silently prays that God will speak into his heart and that he soon will understand how blessed they are to be His servants.

Mary is with child, he says over and over to himself as he walks, not knowing where. *What will our families think? The people will think that we ...*

Suddenly he realizes that he must have been walking in circles because he finds himself at the far end of the village. He finds shade in an olive grove and sits down because he is not only emotionally tired but physically tired as well. Here, in the cool shade, he opens his heart to God:

Hear my prayer Father, for you know what has just happened to Mary. You have decided to use her for a purpose that I do not understand and I am confused. You know how much I love her... we have been engaged to be married and now this... I don't know what to do. I don't want to embarrass her or disgrace her... please...please help me to make the right decisions. We are your servants and will obey you. Amen

Joseph then falls asleep.

He has no idea how long he slept except that it is dark when he awakes. He looks around and sees no one. He realizes that he is somewhat physically rested, but emotionally, he still aches.

He recalls his prayer to God, but the answers are not in his heart yet, so he gets up and starts for home.

When he arrives Joseph briefly stops to say good night. "Mother and Father, I'm home. How was your day?" He asks.

"It was fine, how is Mary?" they both ask.

Not knowing how to respond, Joseph says, "Do you mind if we talk tomorrow about the wedding? I have a lot on my mind now and I need some quiet time up on the roof."

With a curious look on their faces, they both respond, "Yes, of course we can."

The cool night air helps to calm him as he looks out over the village. The view is very tranquil as Joseph looks at the homes scattered throughout the valley. On many roofs he can see families resting and enjoying their time together. But again his thoughts return to his conversation with Mary, and he is afraid he is going to lose her.

They had both looked forward to so much—just being together, raising a family, telling their children stories as they too would enjoy time together on their roof. These thoughts cause Joseph to once again turn to God for peace in his heart. After his prayers, he remains silent for a while as he gazes at God's starry heaven.

By now, the late-evening hour has caused people to leave their rooftops for their beds and he too is feeling tired, so he descends the stairs and retires to his bed, hoping to turn off his mind and sleep. However, sleep doesn't come easy for Joseph, and even when it does, it is not restful because he still wrestles with his problem of what will become of his relationship with Mary.

Then an angel of the Lord appears to him in his dream and says, "Joseph, son of David, do not be afraid to take Mary home as your wife because what is conceived in her is from the Holy Spirit. She will give birth to a son, and you are to give him the name Jesus because he will save his people from their sins."

Suddenly, it is morning, and Joseph wakes from his sleep, rested and at peace, for he has received his answer and will obey God. After he gets dressed, he goes out to the stable to care for Abner, his donkey. While feeding and watering his helpful friend, he is suddenly aware of how everything once again seems peaceful.

The sun has come up and there is a gentle breeze as he walks Abner to his pen. There he pauses to thank

God for telling him that he need not lose Mary, for she will need him now more than ever. However, he realizes there will still be talk about the child she carries. But with God's help they will face it. Then he returns to the house to have the morning meal with his parents.

While they eat, Joseph says to them, "Mary has received word that her cousin, Elizabeth, who lives in Hebron, is with child, and she is leaving tomorrow to go and be with her during her final three months of pregnancy. So later this morning, I am going over to help her get ready for the trip and right now, I'm not sure what this does to our wedding plans."

"Is she going alone? Won't that be dangerous?" his mother asks.

"I'm sure that Joachim and Anna will provide someone to accompany her," he responds.

After he finishes eating, he goes to his shop and checks his supply of wood and things he will need to fill the customer orders he has for tables and benches. Then he remembers that Nathan and Ruth have ordered a cabinet, but he will first need to go by their home so they can decide on the type of wood and finish they want.

Thankfully, he realizes he will be busy for several weeks filling all his orders while Mary is away. But he knows he will miss her terribly.

Tt is still early morning as Joseph heads for Mary's house, where she is waiting anxiously for him to arrive. When she sees him coming down the street, she runs to him, and as she draws closer, she can see a large grin on his face. So with great enthusiasm, she throws herself into his waiting arms, shouting, "Joseph, Joseph, you understand! I love you! I love you!" By the look on Joseph's face, Mary knows her prayer has been answered!

After a long embrace, Joseph takes her hands in his and says, "Mary, an angel spoke to me last night in my dream, and he told me to not be afraid to take you as my wife. He also told me that you have conceived a child by the Holy Spirit. Oh, Mary, the angel said that you have been blessed and we are to call the baby Jesus."

"Now I understand why you looked so different yesterday. You had an angelic glow that radiated throughout you," he says with a grin.

"But then the angel said something that I don't understand. He said that the child will save his people from their sins. Do you know what that means?" he asks.

"Oh, Joseph, there is so much that we need to talk about because the angel that spoke to me also mentioned a number of things that I can only ponder in my heart now, hoping that the answers will come eventually."

"Yes, we do have a lot to talk about ... so let's find a quiet spot where we can share our thoughts and questions," Joseph replies.

They turn and walk through the village to the olive grove that Joseph stopped at the day before. When they find a comfortable place, they sit down in the shade.

Joseph starts the conversation by saying, "Mary, before we try to understand everything the angel told us, we need to be obedient to God first."

"What do you mean?" she asks.

"Mary, we need to be married before you leave to see your cousin, Elizabeth," he says.

Immediately Mary breaks out in a big smile and says, "Oh Joseph, yes! But how can we arrange that on such short notice?"

"I will speak to Rabbi Levi this morning, but before I do, Mary, we must realize that your condition is something that we cannot hide from our parents so I feel we should tell them about our experiences with the angels and that we have decided to be married today."

For a few moments Mary ponders Joseph's suggestion and then says, "Yes, I think it is best if we tell them that I am expecting a special child from God and trust that God will help them understand."

"I'm glad you feel that way because yesterday your father asked me what had happened to you that changed you."

"Mother and Father have both been watching me closely since yesterday afternoon." She tells him.

"If you think it is OK, I will stop and see Rabbi Levi on my way home and tell him that we will have our parents with us for the ceremony so they can give their approval."

"Yes, that is a good idea and if we can be married after dinner that will give us time to explain everything to our parents and meet at the synagogue."

"Rabbi Levi and I are good friends, I'm sure he will accommodate us." Joseph says.

Mary cannot contain her joy as she reaches out to Joseph and holds him close for a very long time. When they finally look at each other, they both have tears in their eyes as Mary whispers softly to him, "You see Joseph, God is with us, and everything is going to work out fine."

Joseph cannot speak the words that are in his heart. He just nods his head in agreement.

With so many things that needs to be done, they start back to Mary's house. On the way, Joseph asks Mary, "While you are away, should I see if we can secure the house we looked at? We will need a place to live when you return, and I will need to build a workshop and stable."

"Yes, of course. I will leave all those decisions up to you … I will be happy living anywhere as long as it is with you."

When they arrive at her house, Joseph hugs her and says, "My parents and I will meet you at the synagogue."

At the synagogue, Joseph finds Rabbi Levi and he is able to convince him to do the ceremony after dinner. Then he hurries home to explain everything to his parents.

When they all return to the synagogue, the rabbi invites them in and performs the wedding and then blesses the couple.

While they are returning to Mary's house, Joseph asks, "Do you have someone accompanying you to your cousin's home?"

"Yes, my friend Leah and her family had planned to go to Hebron in a few days to see their relatives, so they just moved their departure date up to accommodate me," Mary responds.

"That's good," Joseph says.

"Please don't worry about me, Joseph. I will be fine. We will be traveling in a very safe caravan."

Joseph feels much better, and now it is time to tell her good-bye because she has a lot of things to do before she leaves the next morning.

As he takes her in his arms, he whispers in her ear, "I love you, and I will miss you."

"I'll miss you too," Mary replies. "While we are apart, let us pray for answers to the questions that are in our hearts about the baby."

Then she reaches up and tenderly kisses him good-bye.

CHAPTER 4

Joseph's Prayer

It is now evening, and Joseph retires to the roof for privacy and rest. The night air is cool, and the stars are brilliant. As he looks out over the village, he can sense a gentle calm lingering in the valley. A warm glow of light can be seen from the windows of many of the homes, adding to an overall tranquil feeling.

Joseph feels a peace in his soul like he has never felt before. It is as if he can feel the presence of God. At last, he knows that he and Mary are in harmony with God, so quietly he pours out his soul in prayer—a prayer of joy, a prayer of thanksgiving, and a prayer asking God to guide him and Mary in the coming months.

When he finishes his prayer, he sits back, and questions for God race through his mind—questions like: What will it be like raising your son? Why did you pick Mary and me? Will he be like other children? What are your plans for the boy?"

He has so many questions, but he knows that right now, he must wait for God to reveal his plan. In the meantime, he will remain obedient.

Finally he relaxes and marvels at what he sees in the heavens above. It is God's creation shouting His glory. He remains on the roof awhile longer, recalling the events that have happened over the last three days.

At times he feels a comforting peace that satisfies his soul and then there are times when he just cannot comprehend how God was able to do so much ... yet it feels natural. Finally he realizes that it is late and he retires to his bed, hoping to turn off his busy mind.

The next day, while working in his shop, Joseph's thoughts continually return to Mary. This is mostly because he is anxious for her safety and also because he feels that the coming three months will seem to last a lifetime. Finally, he forces himself to concentrate on his work. As he starts to plane a board in preparation to construct a bench, the smell of the wood shavings returns his thoughts to the joy of his work.

That afternoon, he hitches Abner up to the cart, and together they leave to get another supply of wood. On the way, he stops and talks to friends as they pass by. Many of them ask about Mary, and he tells them she is visiting a cousin in Hebron.

After securing his supplies, Joseph goes by Nathan and Ruth's house so Ruth can select the wood and finish she wants for the new cabinet they asked him to build. Nathan and Joseph visit while Ruth looks over her options.

Finally, she turns to Nathan and says, "I like this wood with the darker oil finish. What do you like?"

"Yes, I like your choice," he says.

"That will make a beautiful cabinet, and I will have it done in about a week and deliver it to you," Joseph tells her.

They say their good-byes as Joseph thanks them for the order and assures them that he will give it special attention.

As he guides Abner home, once again Joseph realizes he is going to be busy in his shop for a few weeks just filling the orders that he has, and this will help him pass the time. However, it is in the evenings, when he retires to the roof, that he has time to think about Mary and how much he misses her. He wonders what she is doing and then finds himself talking out loud to her, asking her questions, or telling her about the cabinet he is going to build for Nathan and Ruth and how they can hardly wait to get it. Then he hears himself talking and he goes silent or whispers his thoughts.

After a while he talks to God and then listens for his voice because he knows that when God speaks to him, he can feel it in his soul and often it is for him to just be patient.

CHAPTER 5

Days Pass Slowly

A week has gone by, and Joseph has finished Nathan and Ruth's cabinet. When he delivers it, they are thrilled with the beautiful finish on it.

As Joseph is leaving, Ruth inquires, "How's Mary? I haven't seen her for a long time."

"She's visiting a cousin in Hebron and will be gone about three months."

"Please let me know when she returns so I can call on her."

"I will," Joseph tells her.

During the next few weeks, Joseph turns his attention to the house he was able to secure. He knows Mary will be happy with it and is glad that there's enough property to put a stable and workshop on it. But for now, the new stable and workshop will have to wait because he needs to start making the furniture for the new house, which includes a bed, tables, and chairs, along with benches, storage cabinets, and also a large trunk. This all takes time, but he enjoys his work.

After he completes the furniture, he starts working on the items they will need for the roof. There they will need stools, another bench, and a couple of chairs. When he finishes, he's pleased with it because their roof also has a great view of the village and surrounding hills. In the following days, he moves all the furniture that he made over to their house. Now he can hardly wait to show it to Mary.

"Mary." He says her name again. Oh, how he misses her. He is so anxious for her to return so he can show her their new home. He is sure she will be pleased with the house and property because there is even enough room for her to have a large garden.

Tomorrow, he will start building the stable.

CHAPTER 6

New Neighbors

The next morning he is up early and tends to Abner, and then has breakfast with his parents. After that he goes back out to his stable and starts hitching Abner to the cart and then fills it with lumber and supplies he will need to build the stable and workshop. After saying good-bye to his parents, they start down the street.

On the way, he sees Rabbi Levi and asks him, "When Mary returns, would you come by and bless our new home?"

"Yes, of course. When is Mary expected back?"

"It should be in the next two to three weeks."

"Good. You just stop by the synagogue and let me know and I'll come," he says as he turns to leave.

"Thank you," Joseph shouts as he heads in the opposite direction.

When he arrives at the house, it doesn't take long to unhitch Abner and put him in the pen he built earlier in the rear of the property. After putting out water and feed for his faithful friend, Joseph returns to the back corner of the property, where he has the stable already staked out.

After unloading the lumber, Joseph starts leveling the ground and laying out the perimeter of the stable. He is pleasantly surprised with how quickly he has it all framed. By noon he has the walls covered and is ready to put the roof on. Then he stops for dinner.

While Joseph is eating, a neighbor comes by and introduces himself.

"I'm Ezra, and that is my home just up the lane."

"I'm Joseph, and my wife, Mary, and I will be moving in soon," he says as he stands up to greet him.

"That's good; my wife Sarah and I look forward to having new neighbors. You must be a carpenter."

"Yes, I am," Joseph replies.

"Well, I thought so by looking at your work."

"But mostly I make furniture and farm tools," Joseph responds.

"Well then, we might become a customer," Ezra says as he starts to leave. "We will stop by when you move in," he adds and then waves good-bye.

After finishing his dinner, Joseph is able to complete the roof and nearly finish the door. By then it is late and the sun is beginning to set, so he gathers his tools and stores them in the nearly completed stable.

As he hitches Abner up to the cart again, he stops and looks back at what he has accomplished in just one day, and he pauses and thanks God for a talent that he enjoys so much.

However, Joseph is tired as he and Abner walk westward toward the setting sun. As they travel along, the shadows grow longer, and a gentle breeze cools the rest of the day. Now and then he can hear a mother calling her children in for the evening meal as a gentle peace settles over the village as Joseph nears his home.

It does not take him long to put Abner in his stall and feed and water him. Before leaving the stable he strokes his faithful friend and says, "It has been a good day. You rest now." Then, as is his custom, Joseph retires to the roof after eating.

Again, he takes time to pray a prayer of praise and thanksgiving ... one he feels coming from his heart and a prayer he feels that Mary is also praying. *Could that be possible?* he wonders.

Then his thoughts go back to the home they will live in when she returns. He can picture them together with the children sitting around him as he tells them stories of Abraham, Moses, and the prophets—people who were faithful to God. Then at night, Mary would sing to them as they lay in their beds. Joseph really looks forward to telling these wonderful stories, along with teaching them the Psalms.

Finally, he feels his aching, tired muscles telling him that it is the end of another day and time for sleeping as he finds his way down to his bed.

The next morning, before the sun comes up, Joseph hitches Abner to the cart and then loads the additional lumber he needs for building the stable and workshop. After eating a quick breakfast, he and Abner are on their way. The cool morning air seems to put new energy into his step as he looks forward to his project.

Although it is early, he stops briefly to visit with some of the men headed to the fields to work in the olive groves. There are even a few women at the well drawing the water they will need to do their laundry and cooking.

When he arrives at his house, he puts Abner in the pen and feed him and gives him fresh water. When he returns to his work, he is surprised to see Ezra coming with tools in his arms, wanting to help.

After they greet each other, Ezra says, "Your project looks like a lot of fun. Do you mind if I help you? I've had a little experience building things."

"Not at all. I welcome the help," Joseph says.

The two men work well together, and in no time at all, the stable is completed, so they stop for a brief rest. It is then that Joseph inquires about Ezra and his wife, Sarah.

"I'm a tailor, and I have a shop on the back of my house, which I built … and Sarah and I have a one-year-old son named Daniel," he says with pride.

"A son, how wonderful," Joseph replies. "We are expecting our first child," Joseph adds with pride—surprised that he just blurted it out. Both men then laugh at their mutual joy of parenthood.

"You are a good carpenter, Ezra. Your work shows it," Joseph says.

"Thank you, Joseph. As I said, I built my shop on the back of our house and enjoyed the experience, but I'm not good at building furniture, so I will leave that to you."

"And I will leave the tailoring business to you," Joseph laughingly says.

They both laugh and agree to let the other do his specialty with no threat to competing with each other.

When they return to their work, Ezra helps Joseph lay out the perimeter of the workshop. This building will be bigger and have more room for storing his tools, material, and supplies.

However, Joseph is surprised that with Ezra's help, it is framed in no time, and by late afternoon, the roof is on and it is all enclosed. As Joseph gathers up his tools and leaves them in the workshop, he thanks Ezra for his help and also for the lunch that Sarah provided for them.

After hitching Abner to the cart, they walk with Ezra to his house, and there Joseph says good-bye to the couple and thanks them again for their kindness.

"I have enjoyed meeting you both. Mary and I look forward to being your neighbors," he says.

"We hope Mary returns soon. We look forward to meeting her ... and I am especially eager to see the furniture you build," Sarah comments.

"Thank you ... and thank you again for your help, Ezra," Joseph adds.

As he turns for home, Joseph, once again finds himself walking into the deep shadows of another beautiful sunset as the orange and yellow hues dance across the clouds. The village is quiet as the merchants have closed their shops, and the men are returning from the fields, hungry and anxious to be reunited with their families.

It has been a very productive day of work with a new friend. He feels sure that Mary will enjoy Ezra and Sarah. Now he is looking forward to dinner and conversation with his parents.

CHAPTER 7

News about Mary

In the days that follow Joseph, with the help of Ezra, is able to complete his workshop. He is pleased with it because it gives him more room to work in and has more storage space. He is also anxious to show Mary their home.

However, the next week goes by slowly, as Mary's parents received word that she would return in about two weeks. Joseph fills his days by completing the backlog of orders he has for furniture, which helps to pass the time.

But as he completes a piece, he tells Sarah, and she and Ezra come over to his shop to see what he has made. It isn't long before Sarah orders a cabinet she needs.

"It will be a pleasure to build it," Joseph says. "For all your help, Ezra, I will make it a special piece that you both will like."

A few days later, Joseph delivers the cabinet, and Sarah is thrilled to get it.

When Ezra offers to pay for it, Joseph explains, "This is a thank-you gift for all your help in building my workshop."

"Oh, thank you. That is not necessary," Ezra responds.

"But it is, because you took time out from your work to help me, and I enjoyed your company."

"And I have gained a new friend," Ezra says with a grin and a handshake.

The following week, on the night before Mary's return, Joseph once again finds himself on the roof, only this time it is his and Mary's roof. That day he had just finished moving most of his personal items into their new home, along with his tools in the shop and Abner in his new stable, for it is his intention to move Mary in on the day she arrives home.

However, he is also aware that Mary will be three months pregnant when she returns and he is concerned that this may cause some talk amongst the town people. For this reason, he wants to seek God's help.

Joseph starts to pray, and his prayer is one of not only concern for any shame that might come to Mary but also one of his complete love and trust in God's plan for them. He continually thanks God for his guidance and also the love and trust that Mary has in him. He closes with the promise that he and Mary will always be obedient to God.

When Joseph gets off his knees and opens his eyes, he can't believe the beauty of the heavens above. It's like God is acknowledging his prayer by displaying what he does best: revealing His glory through his creation.

Never before were the heavens so brilliant. Never before has Joseph seen so many stars blazing through the sky leaving trails. It's like God is celebrating, and never before has Joseph felt so close to God.

CHAPTER 8

Mary's Return

The next morning, Joseph wakes up happy and quickly does his chores and hurries over to Mary's house to see if she has returned home.

When he arrives, he isn't disappointed because she saw him coming down the street and runs into his arms.

With tears of joy in their eyes, they head for a quiet place to talk at the olive grove at the far end of the village. It is the same olive grove where they had shared time together discussing their future before Mary left for Hebron.

When they arrive, they find a nice shady place to sit, and Mary in her excitement goes first and asks,

"Joseph, do you remember when the angel visited me and told me that Elizabeth would have a son?"

"Yes."

"Well, Elizabeth's husband, Zechariah, was also visited by the angel Gabriel, and when he told him that Elizabeth would have a son, Zechariah had some doubt about it because of their age. Because of his doubt, the angel told him he would not be able to speak again until the child was born."

"You mean he couldn't say anything?" Joseph asks.

"That's right," Mary answers. "But, when the child was born, they asked what the child's name was. Zechariah could speak again and told everyone that his name was John, as he was instructed to do by the angel."

Mary pauses for a moment, takes Joseph's hand in hers, and then continues. "The angel also said that John would be a man of the spirit and the power of Elijah ... and that he would prepare the people for the coming of the Lord!"

"Did you say the prophet Elijah? What does it mean, 'he would prepare people?'" Joseph asks.

"Yes, the prophet, and Joseph, I don't understand what any of this means, but it has something to do with the baby I carry because when I arrived and Elizabeth greeted me, she said her baby leaped in her womb."

"Leaped in her womb?"

"Yes, she could feel her baby move like it was excited. Also, when I arrived at their home, Elizabeth was filled with the Holy Spirit and exclaimed to me in a loud voice, 'Blessed are you among women, and blessed is the child you will bear!'

"But that is not all, Joseph," Mary continues. "Then Elizabeth asked me, 'Why am I so favored, that the mother of my Lord should come to me?' Why would she call me the mother of her Lord? I don't understand."

Joseph smiles at her and takes a moment just to look at her because once again, he can see a radiance about her that is indescribable.

When he regains his thoughts, he says to her, "Mary, you have been blessed, and there must be some connection between the two children that God plans to use. Whatever it is, we can only trust in God

Joseph

and pray that someday he will reveal to us his plan for the child."

They are both silent for a while, each trying to understand what God's plan could be as a gentle breeze wafts through the grove. Then Joseph breaks the silence by asking, "Mary, did your parents question you regarding your pregnancy when you returned?"

"Yes they did, and I told them again that we are expecting a special child whom God is blessing and we have to wait and trust that God will eventually tell us what His plan is for him." Mary replies.

"That's wonderful. I will tell my parents the same thing if they ask." Still holding her hands, he adds, "I missed you very much, and I never want to be separated from you again, so last night, Mary, I prayed to God and asked him to be with us in the coming months so we might come to understand his plan and that we will be obedient to him."

With a smile on her face, she says, "Joseph, I prayed that same prayer last night, and when I finished, I looked into his heavens and saw the most beautiful display of his creation I have ever seen. It was like God was celebrating."

Then she adds, "Oh, Joseph, I have never felt so close to God as I do now."

"Mary, I too saw that same celebration after my prayer, and I feel the same way as you."

They both laugh and embrace.

CHAPTER 9

Their New Home

As they walk back to Mary's house from the olive grove, Joseph says to her, "I was able to secure the house we looked at, and the owner reduced the rental charge to us because I would be building a stable and workshop on it."

"That is just fine, and you were able to complete both the stable and the workshop?" she asks.

"Yes, with the help of our new neighbor, Ezra. He and his wife, Sarah, live a few houses from us, and they have a one-year-old son named Daniel."

"Then our child will have someone to play, with and I will have a new friend to visit with," Mary comments.

"Yes ... and our home has a nice roof and a beautiful view of the valley."

Mary is excited to hear all the news about their home and neighbors, and then she asks Joseph, "When can we move in?"

"Today, if you want to."

With a smile she says, "Good! While I start packing my things, you go get Abner and the cart."

"Okay, I'll be right back," he replies.

Mary kisses him tenderly before she turns to go back into the house. After the kiss, it takes Joseph a moment to remember that Abner and the cart are at their house. In his excitement, he runs all the way there, and it doesn't take him long to hitch Abner to the cart. "Come on Abner we have work to do today." Joseph says.

To Mary's surprise, they are back in no time.

As Joseph moves his cart near the door, Joachim and Anna come out to see their son-in-law. They hug him and say they are looking forward to being grandparents. Then they help him load the cart with the personal items Mary is taking, along with a few pieces of furniture her parents gave her. It doesn't take long before the cart is loaded, and they are soon on their way.

When they arrive, it is late afternoon. Joseph starts to unload the cart while Mary runs into the house to see what Joseph had done in furnishing it. She is very pleased with everything Joseph has made. The furniture she brought also fits in perfectly. Then Joseph takes her outside and shows her the workshop and stable he and Ezra built.

"Oh Joseph, everything is beautiful. You and Ezra were busy. The house, the furniture, and the new buildings are just what I pictured that we would have to start our lives together."

As tears start to well up in her eyes, Joseph just takes her in his arms and says, "We are home! Let's thank God for that." So they bow and thank God for bringing them safely together.

After a quiet, intimate dinner, the couple retires to the roof because Joseph is anxious to show Mary the view of the village and the valley. It is a perfect night as Joseph takes Mary into his arms and points out various places and things of interest that seem far away but that are still visible from their vantage point.

"Look, to the right is the synagogue, along with the village square, and the well. And Mary, just look at all the other families enjoying the same view from their rooftops," Joseph points out.

"Oh yes, I can see them now, and we will all enjoy the quiet beauty of the village." she says.

Then he turns her toward himself and says, "Just imagine how much we will be able to enjoy our children here. I can see us now, sitting and enjoying the cool night air as I tell them stories of Abraham and Moses. Our evenings can end with you singing songs to the children. Can't you just see it, Mary?"

By now, Mary is so happy and content that she can only shake her head in agreement with a tear in her eye as she lays her head on her Joseph's chest. They spend the rest of the evening quietly, just gazing at God's creation, both feeling a real harmony in their lives.

Later that night as they retire to their bed, Mary snuggles up to Joseph and says to him, "Joseph, God has blessed us both. I am blessed to carry his son, and you are blessed to be the perfect father that he will need here on earth."

Then she closes her eyes and falls asleep.

CHAPTER 10

They Go Exploring

The next morning the sun breaks through the window of their bedroom with rays beaming to the floor. Joseph kisses his new wife good morning and quickly gets dressed and goes outside to tend to Abner. After filling the feed pouch and putting fresh water in the trough, Joseph opens the door to his pen so his faithful friend can graze.

"You rest today, we don't have any work for you." Joseph tells Abner as he scratches his ear. Then he pauses and notices how beautiful the day is as he gazes about the valley. The sun is shining bright through a cloudless blue sky as a gentle breeze ruffles his hair.

After he washes up, he returns to the house, where he finds Mary preparing the morning meal. As they eat Joseph suggests, "Maybe we should just spend our time today exploring our new neighborhood and maybe even take a walk through the nearby hills."

"That's a good idea," Mary says. "And I will prepare us a lunch to take."

A short time later they start out on their journey hand in hand. First they walk through the village, greeting and briefly chatting with people they meet. Mary is happy to be back and to see many of her friends. Some inquire about her cousin, Elizabeth, so she tells them about their new son and how happy they are to be new parents.

When they reach the edge of the village, they head for the nearby hills, and Joseph is constantly alert to make sure Mary doesn't overdo it, so they stop frequently to rest and take in the view. It is very peaceful where they stop. They can look out over the hills and see the many olive and date groves, along with sheep grazing.

By late morning they have followed a trail up one of the high hills, and they stop again to rest. As Mary looks to the west, she points out, "There, do you see that trail? There is a caravan traveling on it. That is the trail that Leah, her family, and I traveled on to Hebron."

"Yes, I am familiar with it because that is the one that our family uses when we go to celebrate Passover in Jerusalem," he comments.

Then Joseph thinks for a moment and says, "Mary, are you aware that I am required to return to Bethlehem in about six months for a census and that is also when you will be due to deliver the baby?"

"Yes, I have thought about it and I will just trust in God that He will be with us as we travel because I need to be with you during that time."

After having lunch under a shade tree, Joseph and Mary slowly start back to the village. From their view up in the hills, the village of Nazareth, sitting on a small hill in the distance, appears very peaceful. As they casually walk along the trail leading to the village, the sun starts to slowly set in the western sky, causing an ever-changing colors of orange, peach, and then darker grays on the clouds.

It is nearly dark when they reach their home, and Mary goes in to prepare the evening meal while Joseph tends to Abner. Abner is very content as Joseph guides him into his stall, and after filling his bag with grain and seeing that there is water in the trough, Joseph finds a brush and starts rubbing and brushing the animal down while talking gently to him. Then he hears Mary call to say that dinner is ready, so he leaves the stable and washes up before entering the house. After he says the blessing, they have a quiet meal together.

"I hope you didn't get too tired today walking in the hills," Joseph says.

"No, I really enjoyed it, especially the sunset."

"Good because I was concerned that you may have overdone it. Are you sure you're feeling all right?"

"Yes, Joseph, the walk and our time together was just what I needed," Mary assures him.

Later, they go up on the roof to rest and enjoy a quiet moment together. After discussing their plans for the coming weeks, they lift up a prayer of praise to God before they retire for the night.

CHAPTER 11

Meeting Neighbors

The weeks pass slowly by for them as they take time to do the little things that a new home needs and also to visit with their neighbors, Ezra and Sarah. While Mary takes a special interest in their son, Daniel, Sarah inquires as to when Mary is expecting her child.

"In about four months," she replies.

"If I can be of any help, please call on me," Sarah says.

"Thank you, I will. I look forward to being your neighbor."

As the weeks continue to go by, Mary is able to care for Daniel when Sarah has to be gone for a day. And Sarah comes for a visit when Mary needs a young mother to answer questions that she knew Joseph can't answer.

In the following weeks, the two couples develop a friendship that sees them spending a lot of time together. They are often on one another's roofs for an evening or going to the synagogue together.

One Sabbath, Joseph and Mary talk to Rabbi Levi about coming to their home and blessing it. They are able to agree on the following afternoon, so Joseph and Mary quickly contact their parents and close friends, asking them to come. The ceremony is not long, but they are happy to have everyone there.

Mary, with her mother Anna's help, serves light refreshments, and their parents get to meet their new friends and neighbors. It is a good feeling for them to know that God's blessing is on their home.

During the next few days, Joseph spends more time in his shop completing the orders he has for furniture and farm tools. Some of the items are for customers in Cana and Sepphoris, which he will have to deliver. On these occasions, Jacob comes over and helps Joseph load the furniture on his cart. Because it will take most of a day to deliver, Mary prepares him a lunch to take.

Also, at times, Joseph is asked to build a shed or a small building for a customer, which he enjoys. But as usual, at the end of the day, after an evening meal, they go up to the roof to rest and talk, and their conversations are mainly about the child Mary is expecting.

Their prayers are for answers to their questions or peace to sustain them and God most often just gives them the peace they pray for. However, while they wait for answers, they continue to be obedient.

CHAPTER 12

Trip to Bethlehem

During lunch the next day, Joseph turns to Mary and says, "In two weeks, we need to leave to go to Bethlehem and register for the census and pay our taxes, I know that we talked briefly about it, but it will be a four-day trip under good traveling conditions, and I'm concerned about whether it will be safe for you to go because your time to deliver is coming soon."

"Joseph, please don't worry about me. I am sure if we take our time, I will make the trip without any problem. Besides, I need to be with you when it's time for the baby to be born."

Nothing further is said about Mary not going. They just proceed to make plans to leave together. The next two weeks are spent with Joseph completing and delivering the furniture ordered by his customers and preparing the house and workshop for their absence.

When the day arrives for them to leave, Joseph loads Abner with their few supplies and then lifts Mary up on his back, and they head southeast out of the valley toward the caravan route that will take them to Bethlehem. They leave with mixed emotions. While they look forward to going to Joseph's ancestral home, they also will miss their home.

The first part of the journey is difficult for Mary because they are leaving the Galilean Mountains and heading south to the Jezreel Valley. As a result, Mary tires quickly because of all the turning and twisting of the downhill trails.

By noon they are in the valley and they stop to eat and rest. Joseph is very attentive of Mary's needs and watches her closely throughout the morning. After they eat, Joseph takes time to wash her swollen feet and then massages them, which does give her some relief.

As he helps her back on the donkey, she says, "This is the same route Leah and I were on when I went to see Elizabeth."

"I have traveled this route every time my family and I went to Jerusalem for the Passover," Joseph replies. "And now that we are in the valley, it should be easier traveling. But if you get tired, stop me and we will rest."

"I will, Joseph."

So they start off again.

Just as Joseph had said, it is easier, and she can take the time to gaze about the countryside, which is a fertile valley, rich in olive groves, vegetables, and grain.

By midafternoon, Mary becomes tired and asks, "Joseph, can we stop in the shade of one of the olive groves?"

"Yes, of course." He directs Abner to a small grove and helps her down.

Then he takes one of their blankets and spreads it under a tree and helps her to it. Gently he sits her down, and she is able to rest her back against a tree, which relieves her soreness.

After he gives her some water, he lays her back on the blanket and starts massaging her feet as she drifts off to sleep.

Joseph

When she awakes, Joseph is lying beside her with a smile on his face.

"Joseph, why did you let me sleep?" she asks.

"Because you needed it," he replies as he lifts her up and carries her to Abner.

But before she lets go of him, she kisses him tenderly and says, "Thank you."

For the rest of the day they continue through the valley until early evening, when they come to the Kishon River. There Joseph stops by the river and sets up a small shelter. As he looks about for firewood, Mary starts to prepare their dinner. After the blessing, they eat quietly and enjoy the sounds of the night and the river rushing by. Once again, God puts on another beautiful display in his heaven.

Before they drift off to sleep, Joseph snuggles up to Mary, gently lays his hand on her stomach, and feels the movement of the baby she carries. Before closing his eyes, he says, "Thank you, God, for this wonderful gift. May he be still tonight so that Mary can sleep."

The next morning, they rise early, and after feeding and watering Abner, they eat and then are on their way. Throughout the day, they are in the beautiful hill country between Galilee and Samaria.

Just like the day before, Joseph continues to watch Mary, only this time she will occasionally walk alongside of him for short distances. This seems to help her sore back. But after lunch she falls asleep while Joseph sits nearby, smiling again at her

The afternoon goes by faster, and Mary seems more rested from her nap. As they near Sychar, Joseph remembers a spot near a small river that he and his family stopped at on their way to Jerusalem in the past.

When they arrive, once again he helps Mary off Abner's back. While he tends to Abner's needs, Mary unpacks the blankets and food for their dinner as he builds their shelter.

That night, they find comfort in each other's arms and spend the evening discussing the baby and what the future will be like. They pray that God will continue to guide their way as they remain obedient to him.

The third day finds them skirting the western side of the Ephraim Mountains, coming into the northern part of Samaria. However, the day seems longer because Joseph can tell that Mary is beginning to tire quicker, so they stop more frequently and are able to find either an olive grove or a date grove in which to rest.

But when they stop for the night, they are in Judea, just north of Jerusalem, and Mary is too tired to prepare the evening meal. Joseph helps her to a comfortable place near the shelter and fixes the dinner while she rests.

Afterward Joseph helps her to the shelter and then starts massaging her sore back as she drifts off to sleep—too tired to pray and too tired to even kiss him goodnight. But it is a restless sleep as she tries to find a comfortable side to sleep on. Most of the night she tosses and turns as Joseph tries to calm her.

The morning of the fourth day finds both of them moving slower as Joseph fixes the morning meal and then leaves her sitting quietly while he prepares Abner for travel.

Before he lifts her up on Abner's back, he asks her, "Are you having child pains?"

"No, but my back is very sore," she replies.

With that, Joseph lifts her up and says, "We don't have as far to go today, and we should be in Bethlehem by nightfall, so we can stop more often if you need to."

As they travel through the Judean hills, they cross the road to Emmaus, and farther on they can look to the east and see Jerusalem, the Holy City, located on a plateau in the Judean Mountains. A little further on, they are able to see flocks of sheep grazing on the nearby hills of the city.

They continue on for about two hours and stop to eat, but by now, Joseph is becoming increasingly concerned for Mary and is glad that they are within a few hours of Bethlehem. As they continue on, Joseph becomes even more concerned. Will they find accommodations in time?

The closer they get to Bethlehem, the more travelers they meet, and Joseph is worried that Mary might deliver the baby on the trail.

CHAPTER 13

Joseph Delivers the Messiah

When they finally arrive in Bethlehem, it is late evening and the village is crowded. They stop at every inn and they are all full, so they continue on through the city to the far side and stop at the last one.

Once again, the innkeeper apologizes because he doesn't have a room to offer them. Joseph pleads with him, "Don't you have anything where we can find shelter? My wife is ready to deliver our child and needs to be somewhere out of the night air."

The innkeeper pauses and thinks for a minute. Then he says, "I have a shelter where I keep my animals. It is actually a cave in the side of a hill near here, and it is large enough for you to put your donkey in and still have room to sleep."

Joseph looks to Mary, and she nods her approval. Quickly the innkeeper goes inside and returns with an oil lamp and guides them to his stable.

When they enter they are both aware of the humid, pungent odor of the barn animals that share the cave, and the animals immediately note their intrusion. Then the innkeeper gives Joseph the small oil lamp, turns, and leaves. When Joseph takes the lamp, the flickering light causes shadows to dance on the walls, and they can see the wide-eyed cattle and sheep staring at them.

As Joseph guides Mary to a pile of soft hay, he can tell that her back is hurting her and her feet are still swollen. He gently lays her back, and as he looks into her eyes, he knows that her contractions are starting. But this mother, who was far from home—far from family, far from what she expected for her firstborn—does not complain. Instead she reaches up and kisses him before he can let go of her.

With a worried expression on his face, he watches her as the contractions grow stronger and closer together. He quickly unpacks Abner and moves him into a stall where Joseph has placed his food and water, but Abner turns to watch Mary. Then Joseph hurriedly searches for something to make a bed for the baby, and all he can find is a small feeding trough, so he fills it with straw for a mattress.

As he turns to Mary, she lets out a scream that echoes off the walls, and he watches her double over. Quickly, he places his robe under her and rushes outside to get water. When he returns with it, it is sloshing out of the bucket as Mary gives out another scream.

Excitedly, he rushes to her and notices the top of the baby's head is about to come out. Joseph quickly kneels down to her, and with sweat pouring down her face, Mary gives one more scream, along with a hard push, and the baby, who will one day save mankind from their sins, arrives! He has just completed his difficult journey through the birth canal and is in his earthly father's hands, wet and slippery.

Briefly, Joseph takes a moment to examine this miracle he is holding in his hands, and with an amazed look on his face, he lets out a sigh of relief.

The baby chokes and coughs, so Joseph turns him over and clears the amniotic fluid out of his throat and nose and then gently wipes the mucus from his eyes and ears just as the baby let out a loud cry. Momentarily confused as to what to do next, he notices that he must cut and tie the umbilical cord, and after doing so, he wraps the child in swaddling clothes.

With an exhausted look on his face, he looks to Mary as she reaches for her baby. Gently he hands the baby to her, and as she places him to her breast, his cries subside. Looking up, Mary sees Joseph sitting quietly with a look of wonder on his face. When his eyes meet hers, they exchange smiles.

Emotionally and physically spent, Joseph moves to her side, leans over, gives her a lingering kiss, and says, "I love you, Mary."

"I love you too."

Then he lies down beside her as the baby's eyelids are heavy and begin to close.

The Messiah is tired.

While the animals remind them of their presence and Abner stomps his hoofs in celebration, the couple snuggles warmly together and rest as they wonder about God's ultimate plan for their child. They know he is destined for something special, but tonight, on this silent night, they bask in the glow of becoming parents while outside the little town of Bethlehem sleeps.

Their rest is not for long as they hear voices and footsteps of people approaching the stable. Joseph quickly gets up and goes outside to check and returns with a group of men.

"These men are shepherds and are here to see the baby," he tells Mary.

As they all enter, Joseph asks them, "Why do you want to see the child? Who told you about him?"

"We were tending a large flock of sheep nearby in the hills, when suddenly an angel appeared to us, beautiful and glowing in a bright light. At first we were frightened, and then the angel said, 'Don't be afraid. I bring you good news of great joy that will be for all the people. Today in the town of David a Savior has been born to you; he is Christ the Lord,'" the first shepherd responds.

Then another adds, "The angel said to us, 'You will find him wrapped in cloths, lying in a manger.'"

The final one remarks, "Suddenly, a great company of the heavenly host appeared with the angel, praising God and saying, 'Glory to God in the highest, and on earth peace to men on whom his favor rests.' So we came to Bethlehem as the angel said and found you here."

Then all the shepherds start talking at the same time about how they wanted to come and see this child for themselves.

"Thank you for coming," Joseph says as he leads them to the child.

As they all kneel around Mary and the child, they say to one another, "This baby is the Lord, the Messiah. The angel told us so."

After spending a few quiet moments admiring the child, they say to one another, "Let's go tell everyone we see about the baby and what happened this evening."

As they leave, Joseph and Mary can hear them talking among themselves about how beautiful the angels were and how bright the light was.

Quietly then, Joseph returns to Mary, and they both wonder as to what had just happened. Why would God announce the birth of their child to a group of lowly shepherds? Then Mary recalls that it was an angel that announced to her that she would have a child conceived of the Holy Spirit.

They decide to keep this event also to themselves and to say nothing, hoping that God will someday soon explain his purpose for the child to them.

CHAPTER 14

Fulfilling Jewish Laws

After Joseph registers for the census and pays the taxes, they decide to remain in Bethlehem for a while longer because Mary is not strong enough to travel and Jewish law requires that the baby be circumcised on the eighth day. Joseph secures a place for them to stay.

Four days have passed since Jesus was born, and it is now late afternoon. There is peace in the village of Bethlehem as the sun's setting causes long shadows to form. Mary and Joseph are seated outside of their temporary home where they are enjoying the view of the surrounding hills. As they look out over the countryside, they can see the ever-changing shades of color cast on the hills by the sun.

Joseph

This quiet time allows Mary to regain her strength and to bask in the knowledge that she has had a child conceived by her Lord. It's an event she does not fully understand but accepts nonetheless. It also allows them to relax and talk. The past few weeks have been very busy and demanding.

At Joseph's urging, Mary snuggles close to him as he slips his arm around her and holds her close. For a short time neither one says anything. The warmth of their bodies touching each other speaks volumes. It is as if they can feel the presence of God and He is saying, "Well done, my children."

The silence lingers for a period until Mary says, "Joseph, I am very proud of you and love you for how you have accepted your responsibility in not only delivering our son but also your willingness to be his earthly father. God will richly bless you for this."

"Mary, when the angel visited me and told me to not be afraid to take you as my wife, God put a desire in my heart to obey Him. He has instilled in me a love for you and the child that I cannot explain," he says as he kisses her tenderly.

Once again they are quiet for a while until Mary turns to him and says, "Bethlehem ... our son was born in Bethlehem. Isn't it wonderful that we are both of the lineages of King David and Jesus was born in the City of David?"

"Yes," Joseph replies. "I believe that it was part of God's plan."

"King David was such a good King; he loved God and obeyed him ... much like you, Joseph."

"God has always blessed me, and life is good when you obey him," he says, smiling.

"You will be a good influence on our son," Mary says as she kisses him on the cheek.

They sit quietly for a while longer until Mary hears Jesus stirring, so she gets up and goes inside to nurse him, leaving Joseph alone with his thoughts.

On the eighth day, Joseph and Mary take the baby to the synagogue, and the rabbi circumcises him.

When the rabbi asks Joseph what his name is, Joseph replies, "His name is Jesus."

During the following days and weeks, Joseph hovers over Mary and the baby. At night they lay the child between them and just watch him as he moves his arms and legs, and they laugh when he tries to focus his eyes on them. But most of all, Joseph enjoys watching Mary with their son. He sits and listens to her as she sings the baby to sleep.

After Mary completes her forty days of purification, she can enter the temple and present their firstborn son to the Lord, as required by the laws of Moses. They travel the short distance to Jerusalem, and when they arrive at the gates of the wall that surrounds the temple, they find great throngs of people there. In the court of the Gentiles, the loud talk of the money changers mingles with the bleating of the lambs.

Mary with the baby in her arms searches the crowd for Joseph, who has gone to purchase the least-costly offering that she might use for a sacrifice on the temple altar.

When she spots him, he has a pair of doves, so together they cross the court of Gentiles and make their way to the inner court. Once through the court of priests, Mary reverently carries her little son up the fifteen steps to the sacrificial altar, where she offers her sacrifice at the fire and holds up her son for the priest's blessing.

When she returns to the foot of the steps, a strange, elderly man waits for her, along with Joseph, who says, "Mary, this is Simeon of Jerusalem, and he tells me that the Holy Spirit told him that he would not die until he had seen the Lord's Christ.

As Simeon takes the baby in his arms, he praises God, saying, "Sovereign Lord, as you have promised, you can now dismiss your servant in peace, for my eyes have seen your salvation, which you have prepared in the sight of all people, a light for revelation to the Gentiles and for glory to your people Israel."

Then Simeon blesses them and says to Mary, "This child is destined to cause the falling and rising of many in Israel and to be a sign that will be spoken against, so that the thoughts of many hearts will be revealed. And a sword will pierce your own soul too."

After hearing this, Mary looks at Joseph, and they both marvel about what was said about their child. They place that in their hearts, along with all the other mysteries about her child.

As they are about to leave the temple, there is a prophetess, Anna, who is very old and never leaves the temple but worships night and day, fasting and praying. Coming up to them, she gives thanks to God and speaks about the child to all who were looking forward to the redemption of Jerusalem. When Joseph and Mary hear this, they keep these comments in their hearts also.

Finally, after fulfilling all the laws required by the temple, Joseph and Mary return to Bethlehem and remain there for a while.

CHAPTER 15

Three Magi Visit

One day as Joseph is tending Abner, he looks up and sees three Magi standing at their door, and he wonders who these richly dressed men are. Are they like the shepherds who came to see their child?

"Mary!" he calls out to her; she will know what to do.

With great courtesy, the three Magi greet Joseph, who invites them into his home. Inside, they find Mary seated, holding the young child. With profound dignity, the three Magi bow down and worship him. Each has brought him a gift, one of gold, one of frankincense, and one of myrrh.

Joseph graciously accepts the gifts and thanks them. Then he asks, "Where are you from, and how did you hear about our son?"

"We are from the Far East and from different countries, but we met on the way as we were all following the same bright star. Our wise astrologers who have studied ancient manuscripts from all over the world told us that a child would be born who will be king of the Jews, and we have come to worship him.

"At first it led us to Jerusalem, where we inquired about where we might find him. But when the people heard this they were disturbed and sent us to King Herod. When we went to him, he said that he would check with his chief priest as to where it might be and then contact us, which he did.

"He also wanted to go and worship the child, he told us. But later in a dream, we were warned not to go back to King Herod. So we followed the star here and will return to our countries by a different route."

After they leave, Joseph and Mary look at each other and wonder why these wise noble men, from lands far away, would travel so far to worship a child. They were not Jewish. Were they given divine guidance? They must have because they followed a star like the shepherds. And why were the people in Jerusalem so disturbed? Was it because the Magi said they wanted to see the one born king of the Jews? They have so many questions—so many things that they do not understand. But most of all, they hope that King Herod will not visit them.

As in all the other events about the identity and purpose that God has regarding their child, they decide to keep it in their hearts and speak to no one about it. Surely they feel that God will one day reveal to them the true meaning of these events and the plan He has for their child.

CHAPTER 16

They Flee to Egypt

Not long after the Magi's visit, Joseph wakes up one night from a restless sleep. He shakes Mary and says, "Mary, an angel of the Lord spoke to me in my dream, saying, 'Get up, and take the child and his mother, and flee into Egypt.' We must leave Bethlehem at once ... tonight!

"Also, in the dream the angel told me that we should stay in Egypt until he tells us it is safe to return, because King Herod is going to search for the child and kill him."

Mary does not question God's instructions to Joseph as she quickly gathers some household items together for Joseph to pack on Abner.

Into the cool, dark night Joseph leads Abner down the southern slopes of the city, and they head southwest toward the Great Sea, as Mary walks beside him carrying the baby.

Their travel is not easy in the dark, even though the moonlight does help them stay on the trail. But the baby continues to sleep in Mary's arms as she walks along. However, by dawn the baby is awake, and they stop so Mary can nurse him.

While they rest, the sun breaks over the horizon, and they are treated to another glimpse of God's heavenly glory as the sun's colorful rays skip across the clouds overhead.

As they continue on their way, Joseph is very attentive to Mary and the baby. He is encouraged that she is regaining her strength, but he doesn't want her to get overly tired, so they stop often to rest, and then Mary nurses the baby as she softly sings to him.

The balance of the day is spent walking through the fertile Judean hills. As they near Marisa, Joseph is able to find lodging at an inn and a stable for Abner.

After they prepare their evening meal, they eat and then rest after having traveled since the middle of the previous night. That night they all sleep well, and the next morning Joseph feeds and waters Abner as Mary prepares the morning meal.

Before leaving Marisa, they are able to purchase food from the local vendors who are just opening their stalls on the streets.

"Today," Joseph remarks, "we should be able to reach Gaza, and as we get closer to the Great Sea, it should become cooler traveling."

"I have never seen the sea … is it as blue as they say, Joseph?"

"Yes, it is, and we will probably see large caravans of traders going and coming from Egypt."

Today they are able to travel with less urgency because they feel safer being miles away from King Herod, and therefore, they enjoy seeing the different countryside and discussing what it might be like in their new home.

When they stop to rest, Joseph takes the baby in his arms and talks to him and make funny faces at him to make him laugh while Mary rests and watches them, knowing that God has blessed her in many ways.

At noon, when they stop to eat, they are on a hill, and Mary looks to the west. On the horizon she can make out the Great Sea and shouts to Joseph, "Look it is blue, just as you said it would be!"

Joseph smiles and says, "I told you so."

After dinner, as they continue on, they come across a number of large caravans headed in each direction, loaded down with all kinds of merchandise, just as Joseph said.

It is late afternoon when they reach Gaza as a cool, gentle breeze is blowing in off the sea. When they enter the city, Joseph secures lodging for the night, and after they have their evening meal, Joseph takes Mary and the baby up on a small hill nearby so she can see the Great Sea.

As she gazes out over the water, Mary leans back against Joseph and asks, "Did you ever think that one day we would be here—running away from some mad king who wants to kill our child?"

Joseph puts his arms around her and the baby while resting his chin on her shoulder and replies, "No, but we can only trust that God will bring us safely through this."

Joseph

They remain in that embrace and watch as the sun slowly disappears into the sea. Never before have either of them seen anything to compare to the beauty of that moment. It is like God is saying, "Be at peace, my children, for I will always take care of you."

Sleep comes quickly for both of them that night, and when they wake up, they feel rested. Then Joseph reaches down, picks up the baby, and places him between them as they spend a few special moments together admiring their child.

When Joseph gets out of bed, he leans over and kisses both Mary and the baby and says, "Good morning. I love you."

Then he quickly gets dressed and goes out to tend to Abner. After feeding and watering him, he gently strokes him and says, "Ol' friend, we are going to need your help for the next few days. We still have a ways to go." Then he joins Mary, and they have their morning meal together.

As they leave Gaza, Joseph asks Mary, "In about four more days we should be in Egypt. Shall we stay in El-Arish for a few days until we decide where to find more permanent living quarters?"

"That's a good idea," Mary replies. "We will require a few days to rest, and it will give us time to inquire about the area."

The next four days go well. There is a lot to see as they travel along the coast and each day, Abner carries his load safely. Often it includes Mary and the boy.

As they get closer to El-Arish, they see more and more caravans loaded with merchandise traveling on the Great Trunk Coastal Road.

When they look out to sea, they can see ships carrying cargo headed for different countries. Never before have they been in such an unusual area. It seems as though they are at the crossroads of the world.

On the day they arrive in El-Arish, they are both excited. As they walk through the town, they look about at the people and find that they do not appear much different than themselves. They stop in the marketplace and inquire about lodging and are directed down the street a few blocks to an inn. After securing a room large enough to sleep and prepare meals in, Joseph is also successful in finding a stable for Abner.

While he unloads their supplies in the stable, Joseph again strokes Abner and says, "You are a good servant, ol' friend. You eat now and rest. You deserve it."

Then they all rest. Even the baby seems more contented.

The following day, Mary and Joseph explore the area, hoping to find a Jewish settlement and synagogue. They are able to contact only a few Jewish families, whom they visit with, who are anxious to hear the latest news from home. However, Joseph and Mary do not tell them why they are in Egypt.

They find out that there is a large colony of Jewish people living in the Goshen Region. These, Joseph assumes, are descendants of the people who escaped Judah when King Nebuchadnezzar of Babylon took them into captivity almost six hundred years earlier.

That evening, while eating dinner, Joseph and Mary discuss their options on whether to stay in El-Arish or move on to Goshen.

"I like El-Arish, but wouldn't it be safer to live in a larger community like Goshen?" Mary asks.

"Yes, it would, and I would be able to set up my carpenter business and have more opportunity to sell furniture there."

They decide to move on to Goshen, but first they will rest because the trip will take at least two to three more days. In the meantime, they celebrate the Sabbath and attend the synagogue in El-Arish.

A few days later, they are up early, and Joseph loads their supplies on Abner, who is well rested, and they are on their way again. They are both excited to get to Goshen and to find permanent living quarters.

As they leave the coastal area of El-Arish, they head south toward Goshen. Once again, they are traveling in a very fertile area, for there are many date groves, cotton fields, and wheat and barley fields, along with fruit trees. There are also small patches of vegetables growing here and there. Then Joseph points out to Mary that this is all possible because the locals water the crops by building many canals from the rivers to the fields.

That evening, while resting at the inn, Joseph and Mary discuss all the things they had seen that day and are looking forward to seeing Goshen because that was where Moses led their people out of bondage to the pharaoh over fourteen hundred years ago.

But now, God is leading them back, and that reminds them to keep their trust in his guiding hands just as Moses had done so long ago.

CHAPTER 17

Life in Goshen, Egypt

O n their third day of traveling, they arrive in Goshen. Because it is a larger city, they are able to find temporary lodging in the area settled by their countrymen.

The next day they spend time looking over the area and are pleased at what they see. They find a synagogue nearby, along with many shops, and Mary is pleased to find many food vendors.

After a week of looking over the area and checking out different places that are available to live in, they settle on a house large enough, Mary thinks, to be comfortable in and still have enough room for Joseph to build a stable and workshop. In the meantime, he is able to put up a temporary shelter for Abner on the property.

On the first day in their new home, Mary is so happy that she can't stop smiling, and Joseph is happy for her. He is amazed at all she has endured. In just a little over three months, she had given birth to a baby under the most difficult of conditions, and then came the visits from the shepherds and Magi—not to mention the angels telling them they had to leave Bethlehem just as they were ready to return to Nazareth. Now, here they are in a foreign country hiding from King Herod.

Joseph thinks that Mary deserves to be happy and contented, so he stops what he is doing and says, "Mary, you are smiling a lot lately. You are really happy here, aren't you?"

"Yes, Joseph. I feel that we can finally start living as a family now. Our lives have been in turmoil for some time now, and I know that we will miss our families, but at least we are together and safe now."

"I'm happy for you. I don't know what God's plan is for us here, but let's make the most of it and continue to be obedient to him," Joseph adds as he takes her in his arms, kisses her, and tells her how much he loves her.

For the next few weeks, Joseph is very content also. He is able to build a stable for Abner, and the property is large enough to have an area for Abner to graze on, along with large shade trees.

Then Joseph builds his workshop, but this time he doesn't have his friend Ezra, who he misses, to help him, so it takes longer to complete, but that is all right. He is finally doing what he enjoys most.

That night after dinner, Joseph sits the baby in his lap, and they play together. Joseph makes a funny face at him, and when Jesus reaches out and try to grab his nose, Joseph makes a funny sound. The boy giggles and swings his arms up and down, all excited. This goes on until Jesus gets tired. Then Mary stops what she is doing and picks him up and nurses him. Often, she sings softly to him as he dozes off to sleep.

When this happens, Joseph never takes his eyes off her or the child, for when she is holding him, there is a beautiful radiance about both her and the child that takes his breath away. Then Joseph remembers that this was God's child, and why wouldn't they have a beautiful radiance?

The next morning, as the sun is coming up, Joseph tends to Abner and talks to him as he feeds him and fills his water trough. Then he opens the gate and guides him to the pen so he can graze. After he closes the gate, he washes up and goes in to eat with Mary.

While they are eating he says, "This morning, I need to go find some lumber and supplies so I can start building furniture and farm tools to sell. I plan to build enough of a variety that I can display them in front of the shop so that the people will know that they are for sale."

"That's a good idea, Joseph. Is there anything I can do to help?" Mary asks.

"Yes," he responds, "just tell everyone you happen to meet what I do, so that I can build up the business."

Joseph then goes back outside and hitches Abner up to the new cart he had made and says good-bye to Mary as he heads for the business area of Goshen. When he finds the shops that sell the supplies he needs, the vendors are happy to hear that Joseph is a carpenter. When he tells them that he builds furniture and farm tools, they say there is a real need for both, especially the farm tools. Joseph tells them where his shop is, and they say they will be happy to refer their customers to him.

As the weeks go by, Joseph and Mary meet more of their neighbors and also people who attend the synagogue. Rabbi Eli and Joseph soon become close friends because Joseph feels he can go to him for advice on spiritual matters when he needs it and Rabbi Eli is fascinated with Joseph's workshop, as are a few other men.

Mary is also glad to make friends and talk to not only the young mothers who live nearby but also the older women who are always willing to offer advice regarding raising a child. With their circle of friends and neighbors getting larger, they are starting to feel like they belong to the community, and this is important to both of them.

But the thing they are especially enjoying now is the changes in the child, because Jesus is crawling and pulling himself up and standing by himself for brief periods of time.

This really gets him excited because when he does, he lets out a yell, as if to say, "Look what I can do!" This naturally brings delight to both of the parents, as Mary reminds Joseph that Jesus will be a year old in six weeks.

CHAPTER 18

Jesus' First Birthday

Those six weeks go by quickly because there is a big celebration on Jesus' birthday. Rabbi Eli, along with friends and neighbors, are invited over for the party. Dancing dominates the day as Joseph picks Jesus up and put him on his shoulders as he dances the traditional Jewish dances, while the women clap to the rhythm of the music, and Jesus giggles and screams with delight. Everyone seems to have a good time, and Joseph and Mary get better acquainted with their new friends and neighbors.

As the family settles down into a routine, life becomes more enjoyable. Joseph and Mary still ponder things in their hearts about the baby but hope that someday they will know the answers. However, they are committed to remain obedient to whatever God asks them to do.

But with each passing day, they find more joy in watching Jesus grow as he starts walking, and shortly after that he is running. He is such a happy child, contented and full of love. He gets very excited whenever Joseph enters the room, but he also likes his quiet time when Mary nurses him and sings to him.

As time goes by, Joseph spends more and more time in his shop. His furniture is very popular with his customers, and there is always a demand for his farm tools, especially ploughs, rakes, and pitchforks.

But now that Jesus is walking everywhere, Joseph keeps him in his shop, to the delight of the boy, who generally makes a bigger mess getting into things than his father does. However, Joseph doesn't mind. He treasures their time together as the months speed quickly by.

During these passing months, they spend more time with their neighbors by going to the synagogue and enjoying all the Jewish festivals. However, they miss going to Jerusalem for the Passover and the Feast of Unleavened Bread.

But it is a special time for Jesus and the neighbor children as they often get to go for rides together on Abner. Joseph delights in walking them through the neighborhood, and even Abner seems pleased to be doing it.

Meanwhile, Mary enjoys her women friends, and Joseph and Rabbi Eli develop a close bond. The two men can often be seen sitting in the shade of a tree, discussing what is happening in Egypt as well as the land of Israel. While Rabbi Eli misses his home country, Joseph secretly is waiting for it to be safe for them to return to their home.

CHAPTER 19

Return to Israel

As the months and years go by, both Joseph and Mary realize that they are getting homesick and miss their families. Jesus will soon be five years old and has never met his grandparents. He has only heard stories of them. They are both praying that God will soon tell them that it is safe for them to return home.

In the meantime, Joseph has Jesus helping him in his workshop when he isn't playing with the neighbor children. He runs errands for his father, puts tools away, and cleans the floor.

During their time together, Joseph takes pleasure in showing Jesus how the different tools work. He is very patient with him as he lets him make simple little items. He also shows him how to be patient and not rush a job when it requires some special detail.

This time together also gives Joseph the opportunity to instruct Jesus in their religious laws and customs and also about their country, Israel, and especially about Nazareth, their hometown and Bethlehem, his birthplace.

But in the evening when the family gathers together Joseph tells Jesus stories about how God created the heaven and the earth and loves everyone he created. However, Jesus is still young enough to enjoy his mother singing to him at bedtime.

Also, at the age of about five, he starts paying more attention to their worship at the synagogue. The reading of the Torah fascinates him, along with the singing of the Psalms. Rabbi Eli is sure that someday Jesus might be a good rabbi because of his desire to learn.

Just a few weeks later Joseph tells Mary that an angel of the Lord once again spoke to him in a dream saying, "Get up and take the child and his mother back to the land of Israel because those who were trying to kill the child are dead."

Mary can hardly contain her joy when Joseph tells her. In her excitement, she throws her arms around Joseph and hugs and kisses him. "We are going home!" she says. "We will get to see our parents and friends again. Oh Joseph, I have missed them so."

"So have I," Joseph says. "Now let's go find Jesus and tell him the good news."

When they find him, Jesus can tell they are excited because they are both talking at the same time. Finally, they are able to explain to him that they will be moving back to Bethlehem in Judea, and later they will take him to Nazareth so he can meet his grandparents. This of course makes Jesus happy because he has heard many stories about Judea and Bethlehem, his birthplace, and is looking forward to meeting his grandparents and also seeing Nazareth, where they live.

When they tell him they will be traveling for days to get there, he grins and asks, "Can I lead Abner?"

"Yes, you may," they both say. "And when you get tired, you may ride him."

"Will I get to see Jerusalem?" he asks.

"We will pass very near to it—but if we don't get to stop this time, we will see it when we go for the Passover Festival," Joseph replies.

"Good," Jesus says, "because I really do want to visit there and see the temple that you have told me about."

A few days later they say their good-byes to Rabbi Eli and their friends at the synagogue, along with their neighbors. When Joseph tells his vendor and supplier friends at the marketplace, they are all sorry to see him leave and say they will miss him.

The next morning, Joseph and the boy start loading Abner with the supplies and tools and all the things they will need while traveling. Then Joseph puts his arm around Abner's neck, gently strokes him, and says, "We have another long trip ahead of us. I need your help again, my friend."

Abner then shakes his head understandingly.

Then, with Jesus leading Abner, the family starts north through the city of Goshen and out into the fertile farm land headed for El-Arish and Gaza. This time, however, the trip is easier and more enjoyable because Mary is much stronger and does not have to carry a child, so she is able to point out to Jesus many of the points of interest on the way, like the date and lemon groves and the fields of wheat and barley.

That night, they arrive in El-Arish, and after they find an inn and stable for Abner, Joseph and Mary take Jesus down to the shore so he can see the Great Sea. For a few moments he just stares at it, and then suddenly, with a grin on his face, he kicks off his sandals, lifts up his robe, and runs out into the water, shouting and screaming for joy.

"Mother, Father," he shouts, "this is fun! Come join me!"

It does look like so much fun that Joseph and Mary join him, and there is a lot of laughter as the three of them start chasing and splashing water on each other. When they finally get tired, they sit down on the beach, out of breath, and watch wave after wave crash against the shore as the sun slowly sinks into the sea.

They are all mesmerized by what they see, especially Jesus, who can only say, "God made this." They agree with him.

That night with the cool air blowing off the sea, the family enjoys the dinner that Mary prepared. Then they say their prayers and retire early.

The next morning is beautiful as Joseph and the boy feed Abner and Mary prepares their meal. The sky is cloudless and the sun is just coming up as they load their supplies.

After they eat, once again Jesus takes Abner's reins and leads the way. Just like the last time, they follow the caravan route called the Great Trunk Coastal Road that will take them to Gaza.

As they continue on the road, Joseph explains to the boy that many great armies have traveled on this route over the centuries. He explains how Roman soldiers marched down this road to conquer Egypt. Then he points out to sea and shows him the ships loaded with cargo traveling in both directions, headed for great seaports of the world.

Late that afternoon, after securing lodging in Gaza and caring for Abner, they go to the beach again, only this time Mary prepares a lunch for them and takes a blanket and lays it on the sand so they can eat and rest on it.

After Jesus finishes eating, once again he removes his sandals and runs down to the water, only this time Joseph and Mary remained on the blanket and watch him play. When he gets his fill of racing through the water, he stops and discovers that there are sea creatures in the water. He is especially fascinated by watching the jellyfish move. Later, as he walks along the shore, he finds a large seashell and some starfish, which he examines closely, and then runs and shows them to his parents.

"Can I keep them?" he asks.

"Yes," Mary replies. "We will put them in a basket and hang it on Abner so when we get home, you can show them to your grandparents."

With a smile on his face, he sits down and they watch another sunset and marveled at the beautiful colors reflecting off the clouds.

The next day, Joseph learns that the new ruler of Judea is Herod's son, Archelaus, who also is very cruel and Joseph is afraid to go there. So they stay on the Great Trunk Road, and that night Joseph is warned in a dream to continue on toward Galilee. That morning he tells Mary about his dream, and after discussing it, they decide to return to Nazareth by way of the coast, which will be safer. When they tell Jesus, he is excited because he will get to see his grandparents sooner.

Travel the next two days is faster because they are not in hill country. The first night, they sleep outdoors in a shelter that Joseph and the boy make, and they spend the evening looking at the stars. This is a new experience for Jesus.

The second night they stay at an inn at Caesarea. There, they are in the foothills of the Ephraim Mountains, and they can see the peaks of Mt. Carmel.

When they leave Caesarea the next morning, travel is slower until they cross the Kishon River in the Esdraelon Valley. However, Jesus is especially enjoying the trip because he is seeing new things and gets to lead Abner most of the time. Plus he sees flocks of sheep and olive groves that he has never seen before.

Now they know that they are almost home. All they have to do is cross over the high hills that surround Nazareth, and there it will be, located on a small hill near the lower valley … home.

CHAPTER 20

Home Again

When they arrive in Nazareth, it is late evening, and rather than disturbing their parents, they spend the night in an inn, exhausted from so many days of traveling.

Even their faithful donkey, Abner, who served them well throughout the trip, appears tired. So Joseph and Jesus find a temporary stable to keep Abner in. After feeding and providing water for him, they brush him down before returning to Mary, who has prepared the evening meal.

The next morning, they visit Mary's parents first, who are very happy to see their new grandson. And Jesus, upon arriving at their home, has his seashell and starfish ready to show his grandparents. They take time to examine and marvel over them.

When Joachim and Anna inquire about their reason for moving to Egypt, Joseph tells them that after Jesus was born, they heard that King Herod was killing children in Bethlehem so they thought it would be safer to live in Egypt. But now that they are back, they are looking for a place to live in Nazareth. This makes Joachim and Anna happy because their daughter and grandson will be close to them.

As they leave to go see Joseph's parents, Joachim tells them, "We have extra furniture and household items that you can have when you find a place to live."

"Thank you, we can use them," Joseph says while Mary kisses her father in appreciation.

They get the same reception when they see Jacob and Miriam; there Jesus receives many hugs and kisses from these grandparents also. They too marvel at Jesus' seashell and starfish.

Then Jacob tells Joseph, "When you did not return after your trip to Bethlehem, I went over to your house and brought back all of your tools from your workshop and the furniture as well. I stored them in your workshop here."

"Thank you for doing that, Father. It will save me from making more."

Mary is pleased to hear that because now they will have something to furnish their new house with.

The following morning, they wake rested and ready to look for a place to live, and their thoughts go immediately to where they lived before. Joseph asks Mary, "Why don't we go back to our old neighborhood and see Ezra and Sarah? Maybe they will know if anything is available there."

"I would love to do that, and I wonder how big Daniel is now."

"If I remember right, he was just past one year old when we moved into our house," Joseph tells her.

"That would make him almost seven," Mary replies. "Let's go now ... I am anxious to see them."

After Joseph and Jesus tend to Abner, they are on their way and arrive about midmorning. There they find Sarah busy working in her vegetable garden, and Daniel is in the tailor shop with his father, Ezra.

The couple is glad to see them and invites them into their home while Daniel takes Jesus and shows him his father's tailor shop.

Immediately Ezra asks, "Are you here to stay, or are you just visiting?"

"We are looking for a permanent home, but we see that someone is living in our old house," Joseph replies. "We wondered if you might know what is available in the area."

Ezra then looks at Sarah, and she says, "There is a larger home with some extra land just a little ways from here that Ezra and I can show you … and we know the people who own it."

Hearing that, Mary stands up and asks, "Can we see it now?"

"Yes, of course," Sarah replies. The two couples and the boys leave right away.

When Mary sees the house, which is big enough to accommodate a larger family, complete with a roof where they can spend their evenings and also property for Joseph to build his workshop and stable, she quickly looks to Joseph for his approval.

With a grin on his face, he nods his approval. He is glad to see that there will be land enough for Abner to graze on.

When Ezra and Sarah see that they like the property, they are thrilled that they will be living close to them again. Ezra takes Joseph over to talk to the owners while the women and the boys return to Sarah's house.

Just a short time later the men return, and Joseph, with a smile on his face, tells Mary, "We can move in anytime."

The two couples are especially glad that they will be able to renew their friendships again, and Daniel is looking forward to having Jesus as a friend he can play with.

The excited family returns to the inn, and while Mary starts packing the few items they have, Joseph and Jesus go after Abner. When they return, they all go back to Joseph's parents and retrieve the cart Jacob saved for them, and then they load up the furniture. With Jesus leading Abner, they head for their new home.

It does not take them long to unload what they have, and while Mary stays and starts cleaning the house, Joseph and Jesus make repeated trips to their parents' house until they have everything moved.

Then Joseph and Jesus make a temporary shelter for Abner and feed him and put water in a trough for him. As they are leaving, Jesus puts his arms around Abner's neck and says, "You were a big help today … get some rest."

By then it is almost dark, so the two of them wash up and go in as Mary has prepared dinner for them. After the blessing, they eat and excitedly talk about all the things they will be doing to get settled. After dinner, they retire to the roof to show Jesus the view of the valley and also the stars.

While there, Joseph watches his son absorb the beauty that surrounds them and asks him, "What are you thinking when you see all of this?"

Jesus replies, "God made it all, and I like our little town of Nazareth. When do we get to go to Jerusalem and Bethlehem?"

Joseph and Mary both laugh and assure him that they will attend the next Passover festival.

Joseph

"However, tomorrow I will take you to see Rabbi Levi and enroll you in his class on learning the Torah," Joseph informs him.

"Good, that sounds interesting," Jesus replies.

CHAPTER 21

They Are Inseparable

Early the next morning, Joseph takes Jesus to the synagogue and introduces him to Rabbi Levi, who then introduces him to the other boys in his class. When Jesus sees that Daniel is in the class, he asks if he can sit next to him, which Rabbi Levi agrees to.

In the days that follow, they are all very busy. Mary cleans and arranges the rooms, along with starting a garden, while after class Jesus helps his father build a grazing pen for Abner, along with a stable large enough to store the cart and the feed.

Next they start on the workshop. But throughout the whole time it takes to construct it, Joseph explains to Jesus how to use the different tools and what they

Joseph

do. With each step in the project, Joseph is very patient with the boy and takes pride in the fact that he is learning.

After each thing is completed, Jesus runs and gets his mother and brings her out to see it. While Joseph sits back and watches, Jesus explains every detail to his mother on how it was constructed and why they did certain things that way. During this time, Mary glances at Joseph with a smile and a wink as she can see the pride Joseph has in his son.

With the completion of the stable and workshop, it is time to ask Rabbi Levi to come and bless their home and Joseph's business. On the day the rabbi arrives, Joseph and Mary's parents are there, along with their friends Ezra and Sarah and their son, Daniel. Also, Amos and his wife, Rachel, along with Nathan and Ruth, are invited to the blessing.

After the ceremony, Jesus takes Daniel on a special tour to show him all the things he and his father built, and then they run off to explore the nearby hills, riding Abner.

As the months pass, the family is very contented. They observe the Sabbath and attend the synagogue faithfully. They also participate in all the Jewish festivals as well as going to Jerusalem for the Passover celebration. Not only did Jesus get to see the city of Jerusalem then, but he was fascinated with the temple and all of the priests.

But now that they are back home, Joseph delights in telling Jesus stories about the prophets of old, which the boy listens to with great interest. After each story, Joseph reminds Jesus that it is important to always be obedient to God. Needless to say, Joseph and Jesus are inseparable.

CHAPTER 22

Mary's Announcement

One quiet evening after Jesus has gone to bed, Mary asks Joseph to go up on the roof with her. After they sit quietly for a while, she takes his hands in hers and says with a smile, "I have something to tell you. I'm going to have a child."

With a surprised look on his face, he says, "Oh, Mary, are you sure? This is wonderful! When … I mean, are you sure?"

"Yes, I am sure, and our new baby will be born in about seven months," she tells him and smiles as Joseph can hardly contain his joy. Not knowing what to do or say, he just reaches over and kisses her tenderly.

For the next few days, Mary notices that Joseph is his happiest, as he walks around smiling all the time. There are also times when she can hear him singing his favorite Jewish dancing songs while working in his shop.

Even Jesus can tell Joseph seems happier, so he asks his mother, "Why is Father so happy?"

"I'm sure he will tell you tonight at dinner if you ask him," Mary responds.

Now Jesus can't wait until dinner. So that evening, as they sit down to eat, Jesus looks at his mother with an, "Is it all right to ask now?" look on his face, and she winks her approval with a smile.

With great curiosity, he turns to his father and asks, "Father, you are smiling all the time lately. Why are you so happy?"

With a surprised look on his face, Joseph looks to Mary for her approval to tell him their secret and she nods her head yes.

"Well," he says, still looking at Mary, "because something wonderful is going to happen in about seven months. God is going to bless us with a child. You are going to get a new brother or sister."

Then Joseph looks at Jesus and nods his head toward Mary.

Immediately Jesus turns to his mother, and he can see the tears of joy in her eyes, so he rushes over to her, throws his arms around her, and says, "Thank you … I really would like a brother or sister to love and play with, and we could go for rides on Abner together."

That evening, while they are up on the roof, Jesus is the one with a big smile on his face as the family enjoys looking out over the valley while a cool, gentle breeze stirs the air.

CHAPTER 23

A Son for Joseph

As the weeks pass by, the family feels very blessed. This is evident in their prayers. During these times, Jesus has many questions he raises with his father about the new baby as they work together in the shop, and Joseph always takes the time to answer them.

Days later, Joseph asks Mary, "Passover is coming soon. Do you feel strong enough to make the trip to Jerusalem?"

"Yes, Joseph," she answers. "The baby is not due for three months. I will be fine."

With a smile, Joseph replies, "I have to admit that I really enjoy Passover more now with the boy than I ever did because he shows so much interest in seeing the temple and the way we worship our heavenly Father."

Again, Mary secretly thanks God for Joseph's love for the child. Yes, Joseph is very close to the boy, and he is beginning to see a change in him—a change that causes him to pause and reflect on those dreams when God was leading them to safety. Often his mind takes him back to Bethlehem and the shepherds who came and told them that they had been visited by an angel announcing Jesus' birth.

And then to think that the Magi would travel such a great distance to worship a child. *Who is this child that I am raising? What are God's plans for him?* Yes, he was told that the child would save the people from their sins ... but how? A child ... how can that be? Then Joseph would be silent for a while and ask God for understanding and guidance.

Joseph is not the only one who is beginning to see a change in the boy. Mary watches him secretly and often finds him praying quietly in his room. Her prayer is that God would reveal more clearly his purpose for the child.

It is now three months later, and the family has been to Jerusalem and celebrated the Passover and is now home again. Mary, with the help of her mother and her neighbor, Sarah, has just delivered a son, and Joseph cannot contain his joy.

With pride he stands at Mary's bedside and lifts the boy up and declares to Jesus, Anna, and Sarah, "His name is James," while everyone smiles and celebrates the new arrival.

In the next few days that follow, Joseph, in his excitement, tells everyone he sees that he has a new son named James. As a result, many visitors come to see the new baby.

CHAPTER 24

Jesus Explores the Hills

During the months that follow, Joseph and Jesus watch over Mary and the child very closely. When they go up to the roof for an evening, one of them helps Mary up the stairs while the other carries the baby. There they glorify God in their prayers for the beauty of the heavens and the peacefulness of the valley they live in.

While Joseph often has a story to tell Jesus about their forefathers and their struggle to be faithful, Mary sings a special song about the love she has for her children, or Joseph sings a special Psalm.

With the new addition to the family, Jesus has more time to spend by himself because his father often cares for James while Mary is busy with other duties.

During these rare moments when Jesus doesn't have anything to do in the shop, he takes Abner and rides out into the nearby hills. He climbs his favorite hill and sits and watches all the wonderful things to be seen from it as Abner grazes nearby.

Often the great camel caravans can be seen coming and going from the Great Sea. Many are headed for inland cities, loaded with silk and spices and other commodities. Seeing these, Jesus understands why he sees so many foreign travelers in the town because they would stop and purchase food and supplies from the local vendors.

Also, he sometimes encounters a legion of Roman soldiers marching by on their way to Jerusalem with their standards held aloft, swords and shields gleaming in the sun.

But the solitude of the area, especially on a late afternoon, provided Jesus the time to pray and seek guidance from his heavenly Father.

CHAPTER 25

As The Family Grows, Jesus Matures

As James grows, Joseph enjoys watching the changes in him. First, he crawls and then walks, and before Joseph knows it, the boy is two years old. Then Joseph puts him up on Abner's back and walks him around the neighborhood so their friends and neighbors can see how big he is getting. Often Joseph puts a neighbor child up on Abner's back with James and listens as the little ones squeal and giggles.

Then, to the family's delight, Mary delivers another boy, again with the help of her mother and Sarah, and this time she insists that they name him Joseph, after his father. Once again Mary can see the pride in Joseph's smile when he takes the baby and shows him to all the neighbors.

Now that the family is growing, they all have more work to do. Jesus not only helps his father in the workshop but he also keeps James occupied while his mother cares for the new baby. He also spends time working in the garden.

But the family continues to keep the Sabbath and enjoys visiting with their parents and neighbors. However, their favorite time together is still when they retire to the roof for an evening, where they enjoy the cool night air and visit and pray together.

During this time, Mary is aware of the changes taking place in Jesus, who is almost twelve years old now. She senses that he is maturing beyond his years because he accepts more and more responsibility in his father's shop and enjoys it the most when his father shows him how to make the more difficult pieces of furniture and farm tools.

He also takes more responsibility with the children. He and Daniel take James and the neighbor children and play with them to allow their parents some time to themselves. However, Jesus never feels that it is his obligation. He does it because he loves spending time with them.

For some time Mary has noticed that Jesus has a real capacity to love, and he is naturally drawn to children. However, she still has many questions in her heart as to God's plan for him. Does he plan to make him a rabbi, or prophet … or a king? Could this be possible? Israel has long wanted a king who would lead them out of Roman rule. But for now, she can only hope that whatever it is, it will bring glory to God and their nation.

Joseph is also aware that Jesus is showing signs of maturing—not only in the work he does in the shop but also in how he relates to the family and his curiosity about their faith and heritage. Most of the time, Jesus raises questions as they are working. When that happens, Joseph stops what he is doing to answer them.

On one occasion, Jesus asks, "Why was I born in Bethlehem and not Nazareth?"

"That is a good question," Joseph replies. "At the time you were to be born, the Roman emperor,

Augustus, decreed that a census should be taken throughout the Roman Empire. That meant that everyone had to return to their own ancestral towns to register for this census, and because I am a descendant of King David, as well as your mother, we had to go to Bethlehem."

"We are related to King David?" he asks.

"Yes."

"Tell me about him and Bethlehem."

"All right, but I am sure that Rabbi Levi has told you about how God made a covenant with Abraham, that if he would serve him faithfully, he would make him the father of a multitude of nations."

"Yes, I remember that," Jesus replies.

"Did he tell you about how we ended up in Egypt for hundreds of years and we became slaves?" Joseph asks.

"Yes, and Moses led our people out of Egypt and they wandered in the desert for forty years."

"Well, after we arrived in the land that he promised us, our people were governed by judges and prophets, and that leads me to the part that connects us to King David," Joseph says.

"This is getting interesting."

"Yes, it is, because it was Samuel, a judge and a prophet, who was told by God to go to Bethlehem, where David's family lived, and find him and anoint him to be our next king after King Saul.

"That is how Bethlehem became our ancestral home. King David was born there and lived there, and if there is ever another census, you will have to go and register in Bethlehem," Joseph explains. "I think I will let Rabbi Levi fill in the rest of story about our nation."

"Thank you, Father. Now will you teach me another Psalm?" Jesus asks.

"Good idea. Let's sing this one written by King David where he is praising God," he suggests.

As Joseph and Jesus are singing, Mary is in the house nursing the baby and can hear them, so she hums along with them.

CHAPTER 26

Jesus' World Expands

Now that Jesus is older they let him take Abner and explore the more distant hills to the west of Sepphoris near the coast. This is just a few miles from Nazareth. He is gone for most of the day, but when he returns, he tells them that he can actually see the Great Sea in the far distance and also Mt. Carmel's snow-capped peaks. And if he looks close, he can sometimes make out the coastal road with great caravans on it.

As Jesus describes all of this to his parents, Joseph responds, "Son, what you saw was the route between Egypt and Damascus. On that road Joseph, the son of Jacob, was taken into slavery to Egypt.

"Also Roman legions traveled it to conquer Egypt and our own nation as well. This was the same road we traveled on when we left Egypt and returned to our home when you were a little boy," he explains.

"Yes," Jesus recalls. "I do sort of remember that trip. It was a long walk, and I got to lead Abner."

"That's right, and you rode him part of the time too," Joseph reminds him with a smile.

"We also ran and chased each other in the Great Sea, and I found a seashell and starfish."

"That was great fun," Joseph recalls.

Then there is silence for a while, and then Jesus replies in a somber tone, "So that is the route that the Romans traveled when they conquered our nation?"

"Yes," Joseph answers.

"I can't understand why any country would want to rule over another country," he says, shaking his head.

Silence follows again, and then he adds, "Now the Romans still occupy our nation and we have their soldiers stationed in our village."

"Yes," Joseph replies. "And that is why so many of our people dislike them and some try to fight them."

This causes Jesus to be quiet and remorseful for a while. Then he adds, "It's not right and should change."

CHAPTER 27

Passover in Jerusalem

Once again, the day comes for them to go to Jerusalem for the Passover. However, this year it is different because Jesus, who is now twelve years old, is considered to be a man in the eyes of the Jewish faith. This time they are traveling with their friends Ezra and Sarah and their son Daniel, along with Amos and Rachel and their children.

The first two days are uneventful as the families travel through the hill country, but when they reach the valley, they start meeting other families also going to Jerusalem and find themselves in a caravan.

However, during this time, Jesus and Daniel are enjoying the trip as they run ahead with other young boys their age, or they sometimes stay behind and lead Abner while Joseph helps Mary with the children.

At night, the three families huddle together around a fire and share their meals while up and down the trail they see other groups of people also seated around a fire, and the aroma of food cooking would fill the air. Later they can hear the sound of music and singing.

By the end of the third day, everyone is getting weary as there are more people on the trail, which slows their progress. Therefore, the children remain close to their parents for fear of getting separated. However, on the fourth day of their journey, as they approach the city of Jerusalem, there are great throngs of people.

When they enter the city gates, it is so crowded that the people are slowed to a crawl, and that creates large clouds of dust as they work their way toward the temple. Everywhere they look there are vendors hawking their products along with innkeepers busy renting out their rooms.

Then suddenly they can hear the priests calling the people to worship with long blasts from their rams' horn. As the family makes their way to the temple,

Jesus shows an interest in listening to the many rabbis who are there teaching, so he remains behind in the courtyard as the rest of the family continues on to worship with the priests.

However, the family celebrates the Passover feast together with their friends and experiences a meaningful worship. This year Jesus shows a greater understanding for the whole festival and is allowed more freedom to go and come. Mary is naturally apprehensive to let go but trusts God to watch over him.

The Passover festival, followed by the Feast of Unleavened Bread, is a joyful and spiritual experience that lasts for eight days. However on the morning after it ends, Joseph and Mary cannot find Jesus.

"He has gone on ahead with his friends," Mary says, so they start on the long trek home.

But when Jesus does not appear at the end of the day, they become concerned and leave the children with their friends and start the long trek back to the city to search for him. Anxiety fills their hearts as darkness starts to set in. Over and over in their minds they try to think of where he might be.

Late into the night, they stop briefly to rest and then resume their trip early the next morning at first light.

When they enter the city, they start asking everyone they meet if they have seen a young boy, and they describe him.

For two days, with worried looks on their faces, they search all the neighborhoods to no avail. At times fear nearly overtakes them and Mary cries, and Joseph reminds her that Jesus is God's child, and they sit down and ask for God's help. Finally after two sleepless nights in the city, they realize they have looked everywhere except the temple.

With hope in their hearts they approach the temple courtyards where the greatest rabbis of the land assemble to teach, and there he is, sitting among the rabbis, listening closely to their lectures and asking questions that amaze the learned men.

With frustration and anger in her heart, Mary says to Jesus, "Child, your father and I have been looking for you for three days and have been worried. How could you do this to us?"

Joseph

Jesus replies, "But why did you need to search? Didn't you know I had to be in my Father's house?"

Hearing Jesus' remarks cause Joseph and Mary both to realize that Jesus is no longer a child. They now have to let him become a man, even though they don't know what plan God has for him. They also realize that Jesus now understands that he had a unique birth. He has a heavenly Father as well as an earthly father. So they return to Nazareth, and Jesus continues to grow in wisdom and stature.

Jesus doesn't forget the experience he had during that trip to Jerusalem. As he sits with his classmates in the synagogue at home, he remembers his talks with the learned rabbis and teachers in the temple.

Someday, he thinks, *I will talk with them again and learn more about the Law and the Messiah we discussed at the temple.*

But for now Jesus is content to learn the carpenter trade from his father. He is happy to spend time at the workbench with him and treasured all the spiritual wisdom he has gained from him.

CHAPTER 28

The Family Increases

Four months later, Mary delivers another boy, and they name him Simon. Once again her mother and Sarah come over and help with the delivery, and Anna remains for a few days and helps with the other children while Mary regains her strength.

As the family continues to grow, Joseph and Jesus work harder to provide for them. They spend more time in the workshop together, and Joseph realizes that Jesus is learning the trade well as he rarely has to ask how to shape or attach pieces of furniture or which tool works the best on certain kinds of wood.

They also spend more time together outside of the shop. They go out into the hills together, where the olive groves dot the landscape. It is quiet there, and they find a large boulder to sit on that overlooks the valley. Sometimes they don't have to say a word; they just let God speak to them.

When they do talk, Joseph tells Jesus how God, down through the centuries, continued to guide their nation and would discipline them, but God never stopped showing his love for them. It is in times like this that Jesus expresses his concerns for what he observes and asks for Joseph's opinion.

This afternoon Jesus has some things on his mind that he needs to talk about, so he mentions them to his father.

"The last few times that we were in Jerusalem for the Passover festival, I saw things that really upset me," he remarks.

"What were they?" Joseph asks.

"I understand that according to Mosaic Law, we must offer for sacrifice a lamb or two doves. But why have they so commercialized the temple area? Don't the religious leaders know that the temple is for worshiping God? It is a sin to desecrate it. The Gentile

Court should not be used to sell these items. They should be purchased outside of the temple."

Joseph thinks for a moment and then says, "You are right. The Temple is meant for worship only, but the one that makes the decision is the high priest and it just so happens that he and his family control or own all those vendors you see inside the temple. And no one dares challenge him."

"You mean he owns all the flocks of sheep and the doves too? What about the money changers?" Jesus inquires.

"Yes, they own them all, and they control the money changers as well. The few vendors outside of the temple are not his, but they have a difficult time getting their lambs and doves approved by the priests inside."

"Oh, Father, that must change!" Jesus says, shaking his head.

"Again, you are right, but like I said, the high priest makes the rules," Joseph reminds him.

After a few quiet moments, Joseph asks, "What was the other thing that concerned you?"

"Do you remember two years ago, as we were leaving Jerusalem, we saw so many men crucified? Their crosses lined the road. What a horrible way to die ... it was terrible. What were their crimes?" Jesus asks.

Joseph can only shake his head. He knows that it must have traumatized the boy, as he remembers that he was very quiet on that return trip.

"Why didn't you ask me about it then?" Joseph asks him.

"I was only about ten years old at the time, and it disturbed me so much that I couldn't talk about it."

"As for their crimes, I can only guess. A number of our fellow countrymen are very zealous about our country, and they cannot stand to be dominated by the Romans. They will do anything to strike out at them," Joseph says. "And when they are caught, they pay the supreme penalty for it.

"However," he continues, "some men are crucified for small infractions like stealing and don't deserve that severe a penalty. Sadly, the Romans can be very cruel, and it is their way of keeping the peace."

"There is a great deal of injustice in our religious leaders as well as the world," Jesus says quietly.

"You are right, and I am glad that you felt comfortable enough to talk to me about it," Joseph replies as he reaches out and puts his arm around Jesus' shoulders and gives him a gentle hug.

They sit quietly for a while and then return home. Joseph is glad that he has had this private time with his son.

CHAPTER 29

Anna, Judas, and Sarah, Complete the Family

As the years continue to pass, the family increases again as Mary finally gets the little girl she has been praying for. They name her Anna, after Mary's mother.

Immediately Joseph takes to this child and treats her as his little princess. When she gets big enough, he puts her on Abner's back, like he did the other children, and they travel throughout the neighborhood. And of course, he always lets the neighbor children ride also, for he loves to hear them laugh and giggle. Often Joseph feels that Abner enjoys the children as much as they enjoy him.

Also, Joseph and Mary can often be seen walking hand in hand with Anna either visiting their parents or resting in their favorite spot, the olive grove, while Anna plays nearby. She also wins the hearts of her brothers, who became very protective of her. They love to spend time playing with her

With the new child in the family, Joseph and Jesus, with the help of James, build two rooms onto the back of the house to give the family more living space, and of course this increases the size of the roof, which they use frequently.

Often on very warm nights, the boys sleep there, and they spend many hours looking at the heavens trying to count the stars, but sleep always overtakes them. During the day, Joseph spends time with James and Joseph, showing them how to tend the garden and clean out the stable, along with feeding and providing water for Abner. After completing their work, they are allowed to take Simon and play with the neighbor children.

A year later Judas is born, followed with another girl, Sarah, whom Mary named in honor of her good friend and neighbor, who was always there to help her deliver her children.

CHAPTER 30

Jesus Grows Spiritually

In the months that follow, Jesus starts doing most of the carpenter work. However, he still calls on his father for advice on special requests for furniture that he has never made before.

Mostly Joseph just sits in the workshop and watches Jesus work or spends time with the little ones, giving donkey rides or helping the boys tend the garden.

However, during these times that Joseph can see that Jesus is different than the other young men his age. He is much gentler, more compassionate, and more mature in his understanding of life and spiritual things—spiritual things that amaze Joseph. This creates a deep love in Joseph for him. It is a love that he can't describe—but it is there in his heart.

James and Joseph are also doing more to help their mother with the house and looking after the younger children. This gives Mary more time to spend with the baby and Joseph. Often they can be found up on the roof enjoying the late-afternoon breeze and watching things that are happening in the valley. Sometimes they walk down to their favorite spot at the olive grove and sit in the shade and talk about how the children are growing and wonder if they will ever know how God intends to use Jesus.

The months and years continue to march ahead. As Jesus ages, he becomes more aware of the unrest in the village and the country. The people are tired of the constant presence of the soldiers, and they resent having to pay taxes to a foreign government, and that causes some to want to rebel. Also, there is a constant dislike for the hierarchy of the religious leaders. The chief priest, the Pharisees, and the Sadducees make it difficult to keep all the laws and still be obedient to God. The leaders also have a sense of arrogance that makes them think they are so much better than the average person. They always want to be recognized for their piety when in fact they do not keep all the rules themselves. They also look down on the common man and do not trust him.

Jesus recognizes this with his many trips to Jerusalem with the family for the Passover. Lately, while there, he looks around the temple and sees the money changers taking advantage of the poor. This disturbs him greatly because the whole atmosphere of the festival is still one of commerce rather than of worshiping God.

He is also aware that he is different from other men his age as he is spending more time out in the hills seeking a quiet place where he can pray to his heavenly Father. This often happens in the early dawn hours as the sun breaks above the horizon, for he loves to be there to watch the start of a new day. Or sometimes he remains on the roof after the rest of the family retires to their beds and just soaks in the beauty of God's heavens. These are all special moments that he treasures. His prayer time is becoming more and more important as time goes on.

He also seeks out Joseph as he treasures his advice and wisdom. However, Joseph is often found teaching the younger children the Torah as well as the Psalms.

Yes, Jesus is beginning to know that God has a purpose for him that was different from any other person.

Mary notices these changes, just as Joseph has, but secretly keeps them in her heart because she feels that soon God will make known his plans for his son.

CHAPTER 31

Joseph Was Obedient

Late one evening, as the family is enjoying the cool night air on the roof, Joseph becomes ill. As the family gathers around him, he complains of tightness in his chest that causes his left arm to ache. Immediately Jesus and James help him down to his bed as Mary hovers over him.

That night Mary and Jesus remain at Joseph's bedside, praying, while Joseph has a restless night. But as the sun shines through his bedroom window early the next morning, sending a ray of light reflecting off the floor, Joseph opens his eyes and smiles at Mary. With tears of joy, she bends over and kisses him while Jesus comes and gently places his hand on his father's and smiles.

However, as the weeks go by, Joseph never fully regains his health, but he is able to be up and participate in limited family activities. Jesus assumes the full responsibility of the workshop and provides for the family as Joseph and Mary spend more time together, often sitting in the shade of the olive grove reminiscing about old times or visiting with Ezra and Sarah.

However, a few months later as Jesus is working in the shop and the other boys are busy in the stable, he hears his mother cry out. When he and the children get to her, they find her leaning over their father, who has collapsed on the floor. Gently, Jesus and James pick their father up and carry him to his bed.

With Mary at his bedside and the children gathered around him, Joseph opens his eyes for the last time and smiles at Mary and then peacefully closes them.

Silence fills the room for a moment as the reality of Joseph's passing sinks in, followed by soft sobbing from Mary and the girls. Slowly, the whole family is consumed with grief as they all sink to their knees around Joseph's bed.

Joseph

After a few minutes of prayer, Jesus and James shepherd the family out of the bedroom as their neighbors, Ezra and Sarah, are entering the house. Ezra and Sarah then direct the family over to their home so they and the rest of the neighbors can assist in the burial preparation according to Jewish law.

News travels fast through the small village as Rabbi Levi arrives to find a large crowd of friends and neighbors outside of the house, all mourning the loss of this kind and gentle man. He immediately goes and ministers to the family even while he too is stricken with grief from the loss of his dear friend.

By late afternoon, burial preparations are completed as Joseph's body is gently loaded on the cart and Abner, his faithful donkey for years, leads the procession, guided by Jesus, as Mary and the children, along with many friends and neighbors, follow behind.

Joseph is buried on a hill next to the olive grove that he and Mary enjoyed so much. Rabbi Levi conducts a very meaningful service, pointing out how devoted Joseph was to Mary and his children and how obedient he was to God. Meanwhile, Abner, his faithful donkey, senses the loss of his master as he stands off to the side with his head bowed.

In the following days, their friends and neighbors are very helpful and supportive as they rally around Mary and the family. But they are difficult days for the family. Everything they do reminds them of him, especially their time together on the roof, as well as those special moments when he led them in worship. They also remember the many times he gave them and the neighbor children rides on Abner, the times spent working in the garden with the boys, and especially the times Jesus spent learning how to be a carpenter, along with the spiritual instructions he taught everyone. These were a constant reminder of the love he showered on his family.

But it is Jesus who seems to grieve the most. Often he is found sitting in the workshop alone praying, with tears running down his cheeks.

One morning, Mary is aware that Jesus is having difficulty dealing with the loss of his father so she goes out to the shop, and when she enters, he falls into her arms and sobs uncontrollably. For a long time Mary just holds him. Then they sit together and reminisce about what a loving man Joseph was.

Even Rabbi Levi stops by to see Mary and Jesus. He too is grieving the loss of a great friend and needs to talk

In time, the family is able to deal with their grief as Jesus keeps reminding them that Joseph was a loving father and always obedient to God.

CHAPTER 32

Jesus Guides the Family

One evening after the family retires to the roof, Jesus tells them that he can't replace their father, but he will continue to work in the shop and provide for them. Then Mary goes over to him with tears in her eyes, and she hugs and kisses him.

The following day, when Jesus goes out to the stable, he discovers that Abner is lying on the ground and having difficulty breathing. As Jesus bends down to stroke him, the faithful donkey looks up at him with tears in his eyes.

Softly, Jesus says to him, "It is all right to grieve the loss of your master. You have been a faithful servant. Be at peace."

Joseph

With tears in his eyes, Jesus holds Abner's head in his lap until he takes his final breath. Sadness fills Jesus' heart as he mourns the loss of this friend he had had for life, and now he has the difficult task of telling the family. It is a sad morning as he, James, and Joseph, along with Ezra, bury Abner on a hill near Joseph, while the grieving family looks on.

A few weeks later, Jesus and the boys find a young donkey to replace Abner. Although they miss Abner, they are excited to train a new friend. When Jesus asks them what they want to name him, their quick reply is, "Caleb." When he asks them why, they say, "Because he seems to be bold and faithful."

In the following months, the children enjoy training and riding Caleb as he becomes an important member of the family. Even the neighbor children enjoy him.

For the next few years Jesus continues to take the family to Jerusalem for the Passover and also celebrates the many religious festivals. But as his brothers get older, Jesus teaches them the carpentry trade, and they too enjoy working in the shop with him.

As they get better at the trade, this allows Jesus to have more private time as he is beginning to get more messages from God in his prayers as to the plan he has for him. The family sees him praying in his room more often, or he goes off into the nearby hills alone and is gone for hours.

Mary continues to be silent about the nature of his birth. However, there are times when she really does feel that Jesus knows but says nothing about it. It was those times when their eyes meet and a thousand words are said in only a brief glance.

CHAPTER 33

Jesus Leaves

Finally, the day arrives when Jesus takes his mother, Mary, to that special place in the olive grove where she and his father spent many hours together. For a while they just sit quietly as a gentle breeze wafts through the grove. The scene is one of contentment and peace. Neither one has ever felt this close to God. Here sits the Son of God holding the hands of his mother, who still has a holy radiance about her as Jesus' eyes smile on her.

As they sit together, Jesus says to her, "Mother, I received a message from God that I am to go and meet Elizabeth's son, John, who is baptizing people and telling them to repent of their sins and return to

God. John is preparing the way for another to come in his place ... Mother, I am that person."

There is a brief pause as a gentle smile appears on Mary's face. She looks at her son and says, "I understand."

Neither speaks for a while until Mary whispers, "I have thought that for some time ... When I went to be with Elizabeth, I knew that God had a special plan for you. And as I continued to hear about John's prophesying, I knew that God had a plan for you both."

"You are right," he replies. "Then you have heard about John's ministry, and you are aware of my special birth ... Therefore I am going to him to be baptized. And yes, God has a plan for me that I cannot tell you about now. However, in the coming months you will be hearing things about me, so I ask that you be brave and strong. In time, you will understand everything."

Both are silent again for a while until Jesus says, "You know how much I love you, and Father will always have a special place in my heart. You both have been obedient to God all your lives, so please remember that our heavenly father will watch over you, and eventually there will be an indescribable reward to those who remain faithful."

Then Jesus bends forward and gently kisses her on the cheek. On that day Jesus leaves Nazareth and heads for the Jordan River, where John is baptizing people.

For forty days after he is baptized, no one sees or hears of Jesus until he and his mother attend a wedding at Cana …

The Beginning!

Closing Comments

With so little recorded about Joseph and Mary, it is difficult to imagine what life was really like raising Jesus as a child. There is no question that God chose the perfect couple to do it.

However, as you can tell from my story, I felt that Joseph was a younger man than most artists depict him. I also believe that Joseph was truly in love with Mary, and he surely must have shown it. This is very important because I feel that God would have wanted his son to be raised in an atmosphere of true family love.

You will also note that I took the liberty to have Joseph and Mary married before she left to visit Elizabeth. This is not biblically supported but I feel that the angel told Joseph to take Mary as his wife and because of that I think Joseph preferred to be married immediately rather than marry her when she returned three months pregnant.

Also, I intentionally left out many childhood experiences of Jesus because I did not want the emphasis on him. However, I am sure that he had very normal childhood experiences with his siblings and the neighbor children. My main purpose was to show a very close and loving relationship between Joseph the father and Jesus his son.

One of the joys of writing a story comes when you have nearly completed it and you discover that you have created a character or object that has become special in the process. This is the case of Abner the donkey.

This was brought to my attention when I received my story back from my friend Charlie Miller, who was proofreading it. His first comment was, "You must give the donkey a name."

Charlie was right because I recalled that another friend, Duane Boyett, had remarked that he enjoyed the part that the donkey played in the story. As a result I not only gave him a name, but as I reflected on this,

I also went back over the story and rewrote many of the scenes and made Joseph more aware of the special helper he had.

I must admit that there are a few scenes that I wrote where there were tears in my eyes while writing them. One was when Joseph died and Abner pulled the cart carrying his master to the olive grove for burial and also when Jesus comforted Abner as he died of a broken heart.

As a result I have become very attached to Abner. I have to admit that I still become teary thinking of him.

Another important aspect of his role is that it has caused me to realize that this animal played a very important role in the story of our Savior. Not only was he a faithful helper to his master, Joseph, but he also transported Mary to Bethlehem and was an eyewitness to the birth of our Savior. Also, he and the other animals in the stable celebrated his birth along with the shepherds.

Later Abner safely delivered the family to Egypt and then back to Nazareth, and he was called on to give many joy-filled rides to Jesus and the neighbor children as they were growing up. Abner got to celebrate many glorious and historic events as he served his master faithfully.

I hope to meet Abner someday and scratch his ear.

CPSIA information can be obtained
at www.ICGtesting.com
Printed in the USA
FSOW01n1249230915
11450FS

9 781490 879857